A Thelonious Monk STUDY ALBUM

Edited
with transcriptions and
biographical and analytical notes by
LIONEL GRIGSON

Parts for C, B♭ and E♭ instruments are inserted

for Jamil, Natasha and Toby

NOVELLO
London and Sevenoaks

Cat. No. 11 0229

Text and compilation ©Copyright 1993 Novello & Company Limited
3 Primrose Mews, 1A Sharpleshall St., London NW1 8YL Tel: 071-483 2161

ISBN 085360 156-9

No part of this publication may be copied or reproduced in any form or
by any means without the prior permission of Novello & Company Limited

The music portions are the copyrights of the company named on the title
page of each piece. Every effort has been made to trace all copyright holders.
Any unintentional infringement is regretted.

Cover photograph: Thelonious Monk in early 1968
Courtesy of Max Jones

German translations by Gundhild Lenz-Mulligan
French translations by Frédérique Normand
Translations ©1993 Novello & Company Limited

The Editor would like to acknowledge Leslie East's key role in conceiving and
developing the Novello Study Album series, of which this is the third title.
Thanks are also due to Stan Tracey, probably the greatest Monk authority,
for providing the correct notes for the 'Little Rootie Tootie chord', and to
Jonathan Dore for checking the transcriptions against the recordings, and
for his help with the proofs.

Contents	Inhalt	Table des Matières

		page/Seite/page 1
Foreword		
Vorwort		10
Avant-propos		17

A Brief Biography	2
Kurze Biographie	10
Biographie sommaire	17

The Style of Thelonious Monk	2
Der Stil Thelonious Monks	11
Le style de Thelonious Monk	18

The Transcriptions and How to Use Them	4
Die Transkriptionen und ihre Anwendung	12
Les transcriptions et mode d'emploi	19

Transcription Discography	5
Diskographie der Transkriptionen	13
Discographie des transcriptions	20

Notes on the Transcriptions	6
Anmerkungen zu den Transkriptionen	13
Notes sur les transcriptions	20

Transcriptions
Trankriptionen
Transcriptions

1. *Misterioso*	25
2. *'Round About Midnight*	31
3. *Little Rootie Tootie*	38
4. *Trinkle Trinkle*	45
5. *Evidence*	48
6. *Played Twice*	55
7. *Crepuscule with Nellie*	57

Lionel Grigson is a pianist and teacher whose interest in jazz dates from his schooldays during the 1950s. From 1960 to 1963 he co-led the award-winning Cambridge University Jazz Band. He has subsequently performed with a number of leading American and British jazz artists including Freddie Hubbard, Philly Joe Jones, Johnny Griffin, Kenny Clark, Joe Harriott and Tubby Hayes, as well as leading his own bands. He currently teaches harmony and improvisation at the Guildhall School of Music and Drama. He is author of A *Jazz Chord Book* (1981), *Practical Jazz* (1988), *Jazz from Scratch* (1991), A *Charlie Parker Study Album* (1990, published by Novello) and A *Louis Armstrong Study Album* (1992, Novello).

Lionel Grigson ist Pianist und Lehrer; sein Interesse am Jazz rührt aus seinen Schultagen in den 50er Jahren her. Von 1960 bis 1963 war er Co-Leiter der preisgekrönten *Cambridge University Jazz Band*. Neben der Leitung eigener Bands ist er seitdem mit zahlreichen führenden amerikanischen und britischen Jazzmusikern aufgetreten wie zum Beispiel Freddie Hubbard, Philly Joe Jones, Johnny Griffin, Kenny Clark, Joe Harriott und Tubby Hayes. Zur Zeit unterrichtet er Harmonie und Improvisation an der *Guildhall School of Music and Drama*. Er ist der Verfasser der folgenden Bücher: *A Jazz Chord Book* (1981), *Practical Jazz* (1988), *Jazz from Scratch* (1991), *A Charlie Parker Study Album* (1990, herausgegeben von Novello) und *A Louis Armstrong Study Album* (1992, Novello).

Lionel Grigson, pianiste et professeur, a eu un intérêt pour le Jazz depuis son enfance, au début des années 1950. De 1960 à 1963, il a co-dirigé le Cambridge University Jazz Band, qui reçut des prix. Il a joué par la suite avec plusieurs artistes de Jazz americains et anglais, dont Freddie Hubbard, Philly Joe Jones, Johnny Griffin et Kenny Clark, Joe Harriott et Tubby Hayes, en même temps qu'il dirigeait sa propre bande. En ce moment, il enseigne l'harmonie et l'improvisation à l'école de musique et de théâtre de Guildhall. Il est l'auteur de *A Jazz Chord Book* (1981), *Practical Jazz* (1988), *Jazz from Scratch* (1991), *A Charlie Parker Study Album* (1990, publié par Novello) et *A Louis Armstrong Study Album* (1992, Novello).

The difference of a 4th in the range of B♭ and E♭ instruments may create difficulties in transferring solos from one instrument to another. Played as written from the E♭ part, some solos contain a few notes above a comfortable alto saxophone range, and so players with a less confident command of the upper register may wish to take some passages down an octave. Another solution would be to read from the B♭ part, in which case the accompaniment must be transposed down a 5th or up a 4th.

Der Umfang von B- und E♭-Instrumenten unterscheidet sich durch eine Quarte, welche Schwierigkeiten bei der Übertragung von Soli von einem Instrument auf das andere bereiten kann. Werden die Soli von den E♭-Teilen aus gespielt, so enthalten einige Soli Noten, die außerhalb des bequem zu spielenden Umfangs eines Altsaxophons liegen. Für Spieler, die das obere Register noch nicht so sicher beherrschen, ist es deshalb vielleicht einfacher, einige Passagen eine Oktave tiefer zu spielen. Eine andere Lösung wäre, vom B-Teil aus zu spielen, wobei die Begleitung dann eine Quinte nach unten oder eine Quarte nach oben transponiert werden müßte.

La différence d'une quarte dans la tessiture d'instruments en si♭ et en mi♭ peut peut-être créer des difficultés à transférer les solos d'un instrument à un autre. Joués comme écrits pour un instrument en mi♭, certains solos contiennent quelques notes supérieures à la tessiture normale des saxophones alto et donc les joueurs se sentant moins à l'aise dans le registre supérieur préféreront jouer certains passages une octave plus bas. Une autre solution serait de jouer à partir de la partition en si♭, en quel cas l'accompagnement doit être transposé soit une quinte en dessous, soit une quarte au-dessus.

Foreword

Following Charlie Parker and Louis Armstrong, Thelonious Monk is the third jazz personage to receive the Novello study album treatment. Compiling these albums has been an instructive experience. Turning to Armstrong after the Parker album, I thought I was in for an easier task. Wrong: Armstrong's rhythmic phrasing proved elusive to capture in notation. Lesson learned: not to take 'traditional' jazz for granted.

No-one who knows anything about Monk's music would expect transcribing it to be easy. The transcriptions in this album are as accurate as possible, but other ears may be right in hearing some details differently. What I have mainly learned from this exercise is a better appreciation of Monk's real originality and integrity as a jazz composer and improviser. His originality seems to be the best kind, which grows from a firm knowledge of the jazz tradition, starting with the blues. The integrity comes from Monk's determination to work only with the materials and in the spirit of jazz.

If this album encourages a wider appreciation of Monk's unique qualities, it will have been well worth the effort of compiling.

LIONEL GRIGSON

A Brief Biography

Thelonious Sphere Monk was born in Rocky Mount, North Carolina, on 10 October 1920. His parents were Thelonious (Sr.) and Barbara Monk. So we assume that the unusual first name handed from father to son was first chosen by the son's paternal grandparents. His equally unusual middle name, Sphere, was that of his father's maternal grandfather.

During the 1920s, Monk moved with his family to New York City. There, he received some private piano tuition, but seems to have been essentially self-taught. By the age of 15, while still at High School, he was already working as a pianist. It was then that he met an important future colleague, drummer Kenny Clarke. At this time, or a little later, Monk accompanied a gospel group for a while. Also during his teens, Monk was associated with the noted trumpeter Cootie Williams, for whom (or with whom) he composed 'Round About Midnight.

By the early 1940s, Monk was working as house pianist at Minton's Club in New York. There, together with Charlie Parker, Dizzy Gillespie and Kenny Clarke, Monk was one of the inner circle of musicians credited with developing 'modern jazz'. By this time, although Monk was still unknown to the jazz public, his work was clearly of interest to his fellow musicians. He was appreciated not only by the young 'modernists' but also by some of the more advanced 'swing' stylists from the 1930s including the tenor saxophone stars Coleman Hawkins and Ben Webster. These two regularly sat in at Minton's, with the express intention of learning Monk's chords and tunes. In 1944, Monk received his first important exposure when Hawkins hired him for a 52nd Street residency and recorded with him. Nevertheless, work remained scarce for Monk for the rest of the decade, though in 1947 he began to record for the Blue Note label.

The early 1950s might have seen a breakthrough for Monk but for the fact that in 1951 he lost his cabaret card over a minor drugs charge and was unable to work in New York clubs. Things went better on the recording front, however. From 1952-55 Monk recorded for the Prestige label, and in 1956, the Riverside album *Brilliant Corners* received good reviews.

On regaining his cabaret card in 1957, Monk was booked into New York's Five Spot Club, for an extended residency with two fine quartets, with tenor saxophonists John Coltrane (1957) and Johnny Griffin (1958). This engagement, together with increasing record sales, provided a springboard for sustained success and for ventures such as the excellent 10-piece orchestra of 1959. For the rest of Monk's playing career, his usual group was a quartet with tenor saxophonist Charlie Rouse. Though Rouse was a worthy exponent of Monk's material, this quartet never reached the heights of the Coltrane/Griffin quartets.

In later middle age Monk left his wife of many years, Nellie, and became the companion of another long-standing supporter, the Baroness Nica de Königswater, although there was apparently no ill-feeling between the two women. In his last years Monk seems to have lost interest in the piano. He died in Englewood, New Jersey, on 17 February, 1982, aged 61.

The Style of Thelonious Monk

Though Monk is always mentioned with Charlie Parker and Dizzy Gillespie as a founder of modern jazz, his melodic and rhythmic style is not at all like the so-called bebop style of his colleagues. The common ground is in their shared approach to harmony.

As the background support for their overlapping solo styles, Parker and Gillespie liked to hear chord sequences which, though often based on those of standard songs, were strengthened by the use of varied voicings, added notes, passing chords and substitutions. Such possibilities had been thoroughly explored in the 1930s by Art Tatum. Monk seems to have abstracted and codified Tatum's harmonic approach and passed the principles on to the boppers. Shown opposite are some of the ways in which a simple II-V-I progression can be re-organized and substituted in Monk fashion:

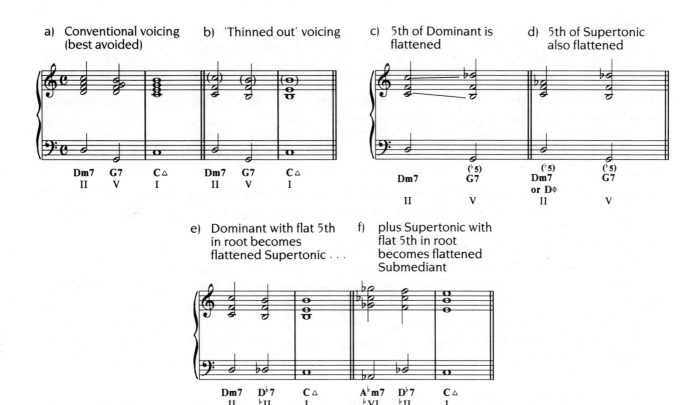

Monk's composition *Evidence*, in this album, shows how an interesting and unusual harmonic/melodic structure can be developed from a simple basic sequence by the addition of flat 5ths and the displacement of harmonic rhythm (see *Notes on the Transcriptions* p.8).

Monk's chords, as he himself stressed, are perfectly logical. But in his hands, the logic of voicing and substitution results in an individual style of harmony whose main characteristic is a seemingly deliberate sourness.

Monk's music shows a strong sense of melodic and rhythmic development which to a large extent may operate independently of harmony. Monk often works by subjecting the simplest ideas, essentially blues motifs, to a process of repetition and displacement that leads to a satisfying asymmetry. This process is very well illustrated in Monk's blues line *Straight No Chaser*, which is entirely developed out of its initial motif or point:

blues motif: *Straight No Chaser*

Asymmetric motivic development: *Straight No Chaser*

The theme of *Straight No Chaser* divides into four phrases, marked above as (a) (b) (c) and (d), of which the first two are nearly the same length, the third is shorter and the last is longest.

Phase (a) runs together the initial motif and one repetition, with two extra notes on the end.

Phrase (b) starts with the motif moved forward in the bar by one beat. The motif is repeated twice without rests; the second repeat is curtailed by one note so as to arrive on the first beat of bar 5.

Phrase (c) is the motif as repeated and extended in phrase (a), but now in isolation and in a new position in the bar.

Phrase (d) starts as a recapitulation of phrase (b). This time the 2nd repeat of the motif is not curtailed but given instead a 12-note 'tail' which leads straight to a final statement of the motif.

THE PROBLEM OF FORM: MONK'S SOLUTION

Typically, jazz performances have consisted of improvised solos over a repeated chord sequence, with a theme played at either end. In the hands of inspired soloists this convenient format may result in great music. But it can also attract the objection that it does not result in a satisfying overall form. At the same time, attempts to impose such form, by placing jazz in a composed or arranged framework, have often stifled the music. Together with Jelly Roll Morton and Duke Ellington, Thelonious Monk is one of the few jazz composers to have combined composition with improvisation so that they enhance each other.

Monk knew well that his soloists were comfortable with the strophic form of repeated chord sequences, and did not interrupt their flow with deviations from this routine. His instinctive solution to the formal problem was not only to compose interesting themes but to make his own improvisations grow out of their melodies and rhythms and not only from their chords. That is, Monk improvises as much on the tune as he does on the chord sequence. His accompaniments show the same concern to unify a performance. Rather than just being rhythmically-placed chords, they are a kind of continuously-varied recapitulation of the theme. In Monk's best work (e.g. *Evidence*, in this album), this approach gives the performance a feeling of constantly expanding from and folding back into its thematic origins.

The Transcriptions and How to Use Them

Transcribed jazz should be approached with caution. The ability to read music and the ability to improvise in jazz style are not mutually exclusive, but they are separate modes of musical activity drawing on separate skills. Simply to read transcriptions, without aural enquiry into the subject of jazz (i.e. listening to the music) is somewhat pointless.

The best results will be obtained from this material by tracking down the recordings. Even if they cannot be found, listening to any Monk recordings will help.

Users of this album are also urged to *memorize* the themes and chord sequences before embarking on the solo sections. Except as an exercise, there is no necessity to play the solos note-for-note (which in any case will be difficult). Rather, aim to substitute your own solos. These can include bits of Monk, either exactly quoted, or paraphrased. The blank continuation staves included in some of the pieces can be used to jot down your own solo ideas (in pencil).

As it is interesting to see how other musicians improvise on Monk's material, some of the transcriptions include solos by his sidemen as well as (or instead of) Monk's own solos. For reed and brass solos, B flat and E flat parts are provided, as well as for all the themes. A part in C is provided for non-transposing instruments.

Transcription Discography

Titles, personnel and recording dates:

Misterioso, 1947
Monk (piano), Milt Jackson (vibes), John Simmons (bass), Shadow Wilson (drums)

'Round About Midnight, 1947
Monk, Sahib Shihab (alto saxophone), George Taitt (trumpet), Robert Paige (bass), Art Blakey (drums)

Little Rootie Tootie, Hackensack, 15 October 1952
Monk, Gary Mapp (bass), Art Blakey

Trinkle Trinkle, New York, 1957
Monk, John Coltrane (tenor saxophone), Wilbur Ware (bass), Shadow Wilson

Evidence, Five Spot Cafe, New York, August 1958
Monk, Johnny Griffin (tenor saxophone), Ahmed Abdul-Malik (bass), Roy Haynes (drums)

Played Twice, New York, June 1959
Monk, Thad Jones (cornet), Charlie Rouse (tenor saxophone), Sam Jones (bass), Art Taylor (drums)

Crepuscule with Nellie, Reeves Sound Studios, New York, 26 June 1957
Monk, Ray Copeland (trumpet), Gigi Gryce (alto saxophone), Coleman Hawkins (tenor saxophone), Wilbur Ware, Art Blakey

RECORDING AVAILABILITY

V   vinyl LP/Vinylschalplatte/vinyle LP
CD compact disc/Compakt Disk/disque compacte

Misterioso – 1
'Round About Midnight – 1
Little Rootie Tootie – 2, 8
Trinkle Trinkle – 3
Evidence – 4
Played Twice – 5, 6
Crepuscule with Nellie – 7

1) *Thelonious Monk, Genius of Modern Music*, Volume 1, Blue Note, 81510 (V)
2) *Monk* Prestige/Carrere, CA 271 68.321 (double album) (V)
3) *Thelonious Monk with John Coltrane* Prestige/Carrere, CA 671 68.912 (V)
4) *Thelonious in Action* Riverside/Carrere, CA 671 68.914 (V)
5) *The Thelonious Monk Quintet* Riverside, 673 024 (V)
6) *5 by Monk by 5* Riverside, OJCCD-362-2 (CD) (re-issue of 5)
7) *Monk's Music* Riverside, OJCCD-084-2 (CD)
8) *Thelonious Monk* Prestige, OJCCD-010-2 (CD)

This is not an exhaustive list of recordings, but a selection of the ones available at the time of going to press.

Die Liste enthält nicht alle Aufzeichnungen, sondern stellt nur eine Auswahl derer dar, die zur Zeit des Drucks erhältlich waren.

Ceci n'est pas une liste exhaustive d'enregistrements, mais une selection de ceux qui étaient disponibles au moment de l'impression.

Notes on the Transcriptions

1. MISTERIOSO

Form: 12-bar blues in B♭
Routine: introduction 4 bars; theme 1 chorus; vibes solo 1 chorus; piano solo 2 choruses; theme 1 chorus

The simple but effective theme of *Misterioso* is built from broken 6ths over a basic blues sequence without passing chords:

I	IV	I	I
IV	IV	I	I
V	V	I	I

Monk carries the melody while Milt Jackson plays in parallel a 6th above. The melody in bars 1 and 3 (and again in bars 7 and 8) includes the major 7th (A) on the tonic chord (B♭). The flat 7th (A♭), which one would normally expect over the tonic chord of a blues, is kept until bar 4, where it strengthens the change to the E♭7 chord in the next bar. In the same bars where Monk plays the major 7th, Milt Jackson hits the flat 3rd (D♭) a quaver later, creating an interesting clash between a 'non-blue note' (the major 7th) and the flat 3rd blue note.

Milt Jackson's lyrical 12-bar solo combines soulful blues inflections with long, flowing bebop lines. His third phrase (bars 3½ and 4) is a miniature study in bop-style phrasing, seeming to show Dizzy Gillespie's influence. Monk's sparse accompaniment reduces the already basic blues chords to rhythmic figures made from root followed by 13th crushed against flat 7th.

Monk's two choruses (the first including an extra bar) have a jagged perversity which makes Jackson's solo seem almost conventional. In a recurrent device (1st chorus, bars 4-5, 8 and 10-11; 2nd chorus, bar 8) Monk seems to bend notes like a guitarist, by sounding the minor and major 3rds together and then releasing the major 3rd while holding on to the minor 3rd.

Other devices in this solo include phrases leading to the flat 5ths of their chords (1st chorus, bar 2; 2nd chorus, bars 1-3, bar 5); and rapid runs based on the whole-tone scale (1st chorus, bars 7, 9; 2nd chorus bars 4-5, 10-11).

After bar 10 of his first chorus, Monk seems to indulge in an extra bar of the dominant (F7), in order to put in the descending figures in bar 11. This puts him a bar behind the bassist, but they are back together by bar 3 of the next chorus.

If there is an objection to the *Misterioso* theme, it is to its rhythmic regularity. As if to meet this objection, Monk plays an effective rhythmic counterpoint to Milt Jackson's line in the last chorus, returning to the original piano line only for the last few bars.

2. 'ROUND ABOUT MIDNIGHT

Form: AABA 32 bars (8+8+8+8)
Routine: introduction 8 bars; theme 32 bars; solo 8 bars (+continuation for student 24 bars; coda 8 bars)

This most famous of jazz ballads was apparently composed when Monk was still in his teens. The version given here is based on his 1947 Blue Note recording, but with the following alterations:

1) The overlapping alto saxophone and trumpet phrases of the recorded introduction have been replaced by a single top line, above the piano part as played. Bars 7 and 8 of the introduction were a double bass break.

2) The theme, taken by piano, is given as played, but the harmony parts played by trumpet and saxophone have been omitted. As played by Monk, the theme soon turns into a paraphrase-cum-improvisation. For comparison, an 'average' version of the unadorned melody has been added as a top line above the piano part.

3) The recording finishes, oddly, with an 8-bar piano solo after the theme. To the first 5 bars of this solo, empty staves and chord symbols have been added to make up a full chorus for student continuation.

4) This version is rounded off with the coda used in various non-Monk recordings of M*idnight*, e.g. those by Dizzy Gillespie, Charlie Parker and Miles Davis. (This coda may be by Gillespie rather than Monk.)

3. LITTLE ROOTIE TOOTIE

Form: AABA 32 bars (8+8+8+8)
Routine: introduction 3 bars; theme 32 bars; solo 32+16 bars (1½ choruses); theme 16 bars (middle and last 8s); coda 8 bars

The *Little Rootie Tootie* theme (dedicated to Monk's son) is an original development of the most idiomatic of jazz devices: the blues motif and call-and-response pattern.

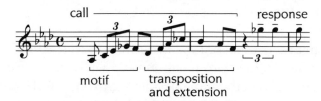

With the last two notes reversed (F before G♭), the initial motif of the 'call' phrase reveals itself as one of the most common of all blues motifs. But in a typically Monkish touch, the 'response' figure is harmonized with a jarring and unique discord:

This chord – let's call it the *Little Rootie Tootie* chord – *could* be described as a D♭ diminished chord with an added F and G♭, but doubtless to Monk it was just a sound.

In the middle 8, the original motif, with changed intervals, is driven through a series of transpositions, over 'difficult' chord changes, to arrive at the dominant chord on the last beat.

The theme's main 8s have no chord sequence or bass line (on the recording, the bass doubles the 'call' phrase). But the corresponding sections of the solo use the familiar 'rhythm' changes (the jazz musician's version of the chords of Gershwin's *I Got Rhythm*). During his solo, Monk's left hand states the chords only now and again; for much of the time they are implied by the bass line. When it suits him to do so, Monk will displace the harmonic rhythm. For example, in bar 7 of the first middle 8, D♭7 and G♭7 get a beat each (beats 3 and 4) instead of half a bar each.

The solo, among Monk's best (it was orchestrated by Hall Overton for Monk's 1959 Town Hall concert), clearly illustrates his improvising tactics. In the first chorus, each main 8 begins with strong, simple rhythmic phrasing on just a few 'obvious' notes. From these beginnings, the first two 8s develop into more complex, rapid phrasing. In bar 5, first 8, a semiquaver motif appears which later is to form the climax of the solo.

After the first chorus, the solo continues for a further 16 bars before the reprise of the theme from the middle 8. The first 8 of the 2nd chorus is a rhythmic manipulation of the flat 3rd (C♭) and 6th (F) of the key, played together as a jangling tritone. In the 2nd 8 the semiquaver/semitone motif from earlier in the solo is worked through 6 bars. The solo ends with 2 bars of semiquaver figures that tumble through 4 octaves to arrive at the middle 8 reprise.

The last 16 bars of this solo conjure, for the present writer, an image of a hyperactive workman, hammering and drilling away at some urgent job around the house!

4. TRINKLE TRINKLE (or TRINKLE TINKLE in some sources)

Form: AABA 30½ bars (7½+7½+8+7½); solo choruses 32 bars (8+8+8+8)
Routine: introduction 7½ bars; theme; tenor saxophone solo; piano solo; bass solo; theme
Transcribed: theme (saxophone and piano parts); tenor solo (1st chorus)

Trinkle Trinkle and *Evidence* (the next piece in this album) represent the work of Monk's two finest quartets, those of 1957-8 with tenor saxophonists John Coltrane and Johnny Griffin.

The *Trinkle* theme is a stimulating combination of an original chord sequence and an unusual, hyperactive melody. The A sections contrast a complex opening phrase (1½ bars) with a simpler figure in bar 3. In the next bar, this figure is transposed upwards and extended into bar 5 to lead to a concluding figure in bar 6. The A-section melody is therefore just 6 bars long. It is followed by a 1½ bar drum break instead of the more usual 2-bar turnaround movement in half-bar chords (I-VI-II-V). But for the solos, the A sections become 8 bars.

The middle 8 (B section) divides into 4 two-bar phrases; the first three each beginning with a repeated semi-quaver figure. The last phrase, in quavers and crotchets, sits deliberately on bars 7-8, with an interesting diminished-chord harmonization in bar 7.

John Coltrane's tenor solo follows the same bass line as the theme. However, Coltrane interprets bars 3 and 4 of the A section as A♭m7 D♭7 | G♭m7 B7 rather than as A♭7 D♭7 | G♭7 B7, as in the theme. This powerful solo is a good example of the 'sheets of sound' style which Coltrane used in this period, in which chords are expanded into rapidly-played scales.

5. EVIDENCE

Form: AABA 32 bars
Routine: introduction (piano) 8 bars; theme; tenor saxophone solo; piano solo; drum solo; theme
Transcribed: introduction; theme (saxophone and piano parts); tenor solo (2nd chorus); piano solo (complete)

In contrast to *Trinkle Trinkle*, which has seventeen notes in the first bar alone, *Evidence* is economical, with just fourteen notes distributed over the first 8 bars of the theme. Most of these are simply harmony notes, one per chord; the interest is in the choice of notes, and in the way that the chords are displaced so as to suggest a cross-metre over the basic 4/4. The middle 8 reaffirms the 4/4 metre by placing a chord/melody note just before each bar.

The melody of *Evidence*, then, 'is' the chord sequence. This turns out to be derived from the changes of the old standard *Just You Just Me*. Here is a comparison of the first 8s of each:

Evidence and *Just You Just Me* – comparison of chord sequences: 1st, 2nd and last 8s

EVIDENCE							
:E♭△ / / Gm7	/ / C7$^{\flat5}_{\flat9}$ /	/ Fm7 / /	Fm7 B♭7$^{\flat5}_{\flat9}$ / /	A7 / / A♭m7	/ D♭7 / /	Fm7	F7$^{\flat5}_{\sharp9}$
							FINE
JUST YOU							
:E♭	Gm7* C7	Fm7*	B♭7*	E♭ E♭7	A♭△ A♭m6	F7 B♭7	E♭

From this comparison, it is easy to see how the first 4 bars of *Evidence* result from the *Just You Just Me* changes by the displacement of the chords marked *, and, in the piano part, by the addition of flat 5th top notes to C7 and B♭7.

The second chorus of Johnny Griffin's long tenor solo was chosen for transcription to show how an improviser may elect to over-ride the apparent complexity of Monk's changes, and instead play with obvious humour over the simpler changes from which Monk's are derived.

6. PLAYED TWICE

Form: AABA (4+4+4+4) repeated
Routine: theme; cornet solo; tenor saxophone solo; piano solo; theme
Transcribed: theme (front-line and piano parts); cornet solo (1st chorus)

This repeated 16-bar theme could be said to be in compressed AABA form, in 4-bar rather than 8-bar sections. It is a satisfyingly Monkish composition, with a tightly-argued motivic development and a strange but not complex chord sequence.

The whole theme evolves from the continuations of the opening figure. We shall label this figure and its continuation as (a) and (b):

a) figure   b) continuation

Figure (a), in a 3/8 cross-rhythm, is harmonized by a common move, C∆ to D flat 7. The D♭7 arrives on the 4th beat of bar 1, and is carried on for bars 2 and 3 as the harmony to figure (b). The last two notes of this figure are repeated in bar 4, but a beat late and transposed to an unexpected chord, A13. As if dissatisfied with this conclusion, the music tries again. This time (in bar 7) the last two notes of figure (b) are not repeated but are immediately transposed to a new chord, Gm9, which lasts for two bars. Will this do? Apparently not. In a new tactic, figure (b) is transposed onto another new chord, a special Monk voicing of F7 with B♭ on top. Over four bars of this chord figure (b) is played three times, at 5-beat intervals, but still cannot settle. In a last effort, the music starts again from the beginning. This time, figure (b) extends itself to find a way from D♭7 through Gm7 and A13 to end happily on D∆. Perhaps the unexpected A13 chord back in bar 4 signposted this eventual conclusion. But now the question arises: is the piece in C or D? We can guess what Monk would have thought about such questions . . .

7. CREPUSCULE WITH NELLIE

As the last item in our introductory Monk collection, a lead-line is provided for one of his most distinguished ballads. If you know that 'crepuscule' is from the Latin for 'twilight', and, of course, that Nellie was his wife, then you will guess both from the title and the mood of the piece that it depicts a special shared time.

Rather than a filled-in piano version, only the melody and chord symbols are given – providing an opportunity for pianists, guitarists and for that matter arrangers to apply their knowledge of Monk's chord style in realizing the symbols. After trying this, a different style of texture could be adopted, say that of Bill Evans (who, of course, had a profound respect for Monk. Evans's versions of *'Round Midnight** are excellent examples of how another stylist may treat the problem of interpreting Monk. It is said, by the way, that when first making his way in New York, he would sometimes stay the night in Monk's flat, where Monk would play the night through for his visitor . . .).

*on the Bill Evans albums *Trio 64* and *Conversations with Myself*

Vorwort

Nach Charlie Parker und Louis Armstrong soll nun auch der dritten Jazz-Persönlichkeit, Thelonious Monk, ein Novello Studienalbum gewidmet werden. Die Zusammenstellung dieser Bücher war eine lehrreiche Erfahrung. Als ich mich nach dem Buch über Parker Armstrong zuwandte, dachte ich, daß dies eine leichtere Aufgabe wäre. Falsch: Armstrongs rhythmische Phrasierung ließ sich nicht in Noten festhalten. Ich habe gelernt, daß 'traditioneller' Jazz nicht für selbstverständlich gehalten werden darf.

Niemand, der etwas von Monks Musik versteht, wird ihre Transkription einfach finden. Die Transkriptionen in diesem Album sind so genau wie möglich.

Gewisse Details mögen jedoch für andere Ohren zu Recht anders klingen. Durch diese Übung habe ich vor allem ein besseres Verständnis für Monks wirkliche Originalität und Integrität als Jazzkomponist und -improvisator bekommen. Seine Originalität scheint von der besten Art zu sein, jener, die aus dem gründlichen Wissen um die Jazztradition – angefangen mit dem Blues – stammt. Die Integrität ergibt sich aus Monks Entschlossenheit, nur mit den Materialien und im Geist des Jazz zu arbeiten.

Wenn dieses Album eine weitergehende Würdigung von Monks einzigartigen Eigenschaften anregt, so war es die Anstrengung der Zusammenstellung mehr als wert.

LIONEL GRIGSON

Kurze Biographie

Thelonious Sphere Monk wurde am 10. Oktober 1920 in Rocky Mount, North Carolina, geboren. Seine Eltern waren Thelonious (Sr.) und Barbara Monk. Es ist daher zu vermuten, daß der ungewöhnliche Vorname, der vom Vater auf den Sohn überging, zuerst von den väterlichen Großeltern des Sohnes ausgewählt worden war. Sein ebenso ungewöhnlicher Mittelname, Sphere, stammt von dem Großvater seines Vaters mütterlicherseits.

Während der 1920er Jahre zog Monk mit seinen Eltern nach New York City um. Dort erhielt er einige private Klavierstunden, blieb jedoch scheinbar hauptsächlich Autodidakt. Im Alter von 15 Jahren, als er noch die High School besuchte, arbeitete Monk bereits als Pianist. Damals traf er einen bedeutenden zukünftigen Kollegen, den Schlagzeuger Kenny Clarke. Zu jener Zeit oder etwas später, begleitete Monk für einige Zeit eine Gospelgruppe. Als Teenager verkehrte er auch mit dem bekannten Trompeter Cootie Williams, für den (oder mit dem) er 'Round About Midnight komponierte.

Zu Beginn der 1940er Jahre arbeitete Monk als Hauspianist für den Minton's Club in New York. Er gehörte dort, zusammen mit Charlie Parker, Dizzy Gillespie und Kenny Clarke, zu dem engeren Kreis von Musikern, dem die Entwicklung des 'modernen Jazz' zugeschrieben wird.

Obwohl Monk dem Jazz publikum jener Zeit immer noch unbekannt war, waren seine Kompositionen für seine Musikerkollegen von Interesse. Nicht nur die jungen 'Modernisten' schätzten ihn, sondern auch einige der fortgeschritteneren 'Swing'-Stilisten aus den 1930er Jahren einschließlich der Star-Tenorsaxophonisten Coleman Hawkins und Ben Webster. Diese beiden besuchten das Minton's regelmäßig mit der ausdrücklichen Absicht, Monks Akkorde und Melodien zu lernen. 1944, als Hawkins ihn für eine

Hausstelle in der 52. Straße engagierte und mit ihm Aufnahmen machte, trat Monk erstmals stärker in die Öffentlichkeit. Bis zum Ende des Jahrzehnts hatte er dennoch wenig Aufträge, obwohl er 1947 anfing, für das Blue Note Label Aufnahmen zu machen.

In den frühen 1950er Jahren wäre Monk vielleicht der Durchbruch gelungen, hätte er nicht 1951 seine Nachtklub-Lizenz wegen eines geringen Rauschgiftdelikts verloren. Er konnte deshalb nicht mehr in New Yorker Clubs arbeiten. Bei den Schallplattenaufnahmen sah es jedoch besser aus. Von 1952-55 machte Monk Aufnahmen für das Prestige Label, und 1956 erhielt sein Riverside Album *Brilliant Corners* gute Kritiken.

Nachdem Monk 1957 seine Nachtklub-Lizenz wiedererhalten hatte, wurde er in New Yorks Five Spot Club für eine längere Zeit mit zwei guten Quartetts engagiert, mit dem Tenorsaxophonisten John Coltrane (1957) und Johnny Griffin (1958). Diese Verpflichtung war zusammen mit zunehmenden Schallplattenverkäufen ein Sprungbrett für anhaltenden Erfolg und für Unternehmen wie das ausgezeichnete zehnköpfige Orchester von 1959. Für den Rest seiner Karriere als Musiker war seine Gruppe ein Quartett mit dem Tenorsaxophonisten Charlie Rouse. Obwohl Rouse ein würdiger Vertreter von Monks Material war, wurde dieses Quartett doch nie so berühmt wie diejenigen mit Coltrane/Griffin.

Im mittleren Alter verließ Monk seine langjährige Ehefrau Nellie und wurde der Gefährte einer anderen alten Anhängerin, der Baronin Nica de Königswater. Dennoch hegten die beiden Frauen keinen Groll gegeneinander. In seinen letzten Jahren scheint Monk das Interesse am Klavier verloren zu haben. Er starb in Englewood, New Jersey, am 17. Februar 1982 im Alter von 61 Jahren.

Der Stil Thelonious Monks

Obwohl Monk zusammen mit Charlie Parker und Dizzy Gillespie als ein Begründer des Modernen Jazz gilt, hat sein melodischer und rhythmischer Stil nichts gemein mit dem sogenannten Bebop-Stil seiner Kollegen. Die Gemeinsamkeit liegt in ihrer ähnlichen Annäherung an die Harmonie.

Als Unterstützung im Hintergrund für ihre sich überschneidenden Solostile hörten Parker und Gillespie gern Akkordsequenzen, die, obwohl sie häufig auf jenen gewöhnlicher Lieder beruhen, durch variierte Intonation, hinzugefügte Noten, Durchgangsakkorde und Vertauschungen verstärkt wurden. Art Tatum hatte solche Möglichkeiten in den 1930er Jahren erschöpfend erforscht. Monk hat Tatums harmonische Annäherung scheinbar abstrahiert und kodifiziert und die Prinzipien an die Bopper weitergegeben. Unten finden Sie einige Beispiele dafür, wie eine einfache II-V-I Fortschreitung neugestaltet und auf Monk'sche Art und Weise vertauscht werden kann:

(a) Traditionelle Intonation (besser vermeiden)   (b) 'Spärlichere' Intonation

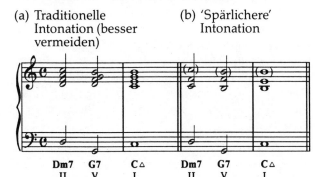

(c) Quinte der Dominante ist erniedrigt (entgegengesetzte Bewegung in RH)   (d) Quinte der 2. Stufe ist ebenfalls erniedrigt

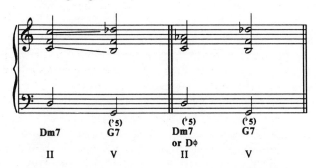

(e) Dominante mit erniedrigter Quinte in Grundstellung wird zu erniedrigter 2. Stufe . . .   (f) und 2. Stufe mit erniedrigter Quinte in Grundstellung wird zu 6. Stufe

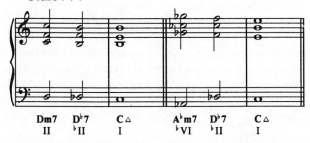

Anhand von Monks Komposition *Evidence* in diesem Album, wird deutlich wie eine interessante und ungewöhnliche harmonische/melodische Struktur aus einer einfachen Sequenz durch das Hinzufügen von verminderten Quinten und die Verschiebung des harmonischen Rhythmus entwickelt werden kann. (Vergleiche Anmerkungen zu den Transkriptionen S. 15)

Monks Akkorde sind, wie er selbst sagte, völlig logisch. In seinen Händen resultiert die Logik von Intonation und Vertauschung jedoch in einem individuellen Stil der Harmonie, deren Hauptcharakteristik eine scheinbar bewußte Bitterkeit ist.

Monks Musik zeigt einen starken Sinn für melodische und rhythmische Entwicklung, die zu einem großen Teil unabhängig von der Harmonie funktioniert. Monk unterwirft die einfachsten Ideen – hauptsächlich Bluesmotive – einem Prozess von Wiederholung und Verschiebung, der zu einer befriedigenden Asymmetrie führt. Dieser Vorgang wird in Monks Bluesline *Straight No Chaser*, die völlig aus ihrem Anfangsmotiv oder -punkt entwickelt wird, sehr gut verdeutlicht.

Bluesmotiv: *Straight No Chaser*

Asymmetrische motivische Entwicklung: *Straight No Chaser*

Das Thema von *Straight No Chaser* ist in vier Phrasen unterteilt, die oben als (a), (b), (c) und (d) bezeichnet werden. Die ersten beiden sind fast gleich lang, die dritte ist kürzer und die letzte am längsten.

Phrase (a) führt das Anfangsmotiv und eine Wiederholung mit zwei zusätzlichen Noten am Ende zusammen.

Phrase (b) fängt mit dem Motiv an, das im Takt einen Schlag vorgerückt ist. Das Motiv wird zweimal ohne Pausen wiederholt. Die zweite Wiederholung ist um eine Note verkürzt, so daß sie auf dem ersten Schlag von Takt 5 ankommt.

Phrase (c) besteht aus dem Motiv mit Wiederholung und Erweiterung wie in Phrase (a), jetzt jedoch isoliert und in einer neuen Position im Takt.

Phrase (d) beginnt als eine Wiederkehr von Phrase (b). Dieses Mal ist die zweite Wiederholung des Motivs nicht verkürzt, sondern erhält einen 'Schwanz', bestehend aus 12 Noten, der geradewegs zu einer letzten Aufstellung des Motivs führt.

DAS FORMPROBLEM: MONKS LÖSUNG

Jazzaufführungen bestanden gewöhnlich aus einem improvisierten Solo über einer wiederholten Akkordsequenz und einem Thema, das am Anfang und Ende gespielt wurde. In den Händen glänzender Solisten mag dieses bequeme Format großartige Musik hervorbringen. Es mag jedoch auch den Einwand provozieren, daß es im Ganzen keine befriedigende Form zur Folge hat. Zur gleichen Zeit haben jedoch Versuche, dem Jazz eine solche Form aufzuzwingen, indem er in ein komponiertes oder vorbereitetes Gerüst gestellt wurde, die Musik oft unterdrückt. Thelonious Monk ist, zusammen mit Jelly Roll Morton und Duke Ellington, einer der wenigen Jazzkomponisten, die Komposition mit Improvisation auf eine solche Art und Weise verbunden haben, daß sich beide erhöhen.

Monk wußte nur zu gut, daß sich seine Solisten mit der strophischen Form wiederholter Akkordsequenzen wohlfühlten und unterbrach ihren Fluß nicht durch Abweichungen von dieser Routine. Seine instinktive Lösung des formalen Problems war nicht nur die Komposition interessanter Themen. Er ließ auch seine eigenen Improvisationen aus ihren Melodien und Rhythmen und nicht nur aus ihren Akkorden fließen. Das heißt, Monk improvisierte soviel über der Melodie wie über der Akkordsequenz. Seine Begleitungen zeigten dasselbe Bemühen, eine Aufführung zu vereinheitlichen. Anstelle von nur rhythmisch plazierten Akkorden sind sie eine Art ständig variierter Wiederkehr des Themas. In Monks besten Kompositionen (z.B. *Evidence*, in diesem Album), gibt diese Annäherung der Aufführung ein Gefühl von ständiger Entfaltung aus ihren thematischen Ursprüngen und von Zurückfallen in dieselben.

Die Transkriptionen und Ihre Anwendung

Transkribierter Jazz muß mit Vorsicht genossen werden. Die Fähigkeit des Notenlesens und jene, im Jazzstil improvisieren zu können, schließen einander nicht aus, sind jedoch verschiedene Arten von musikalischer Aktivität, die auf verschiedene Fertigkeiten zurückgreifen. Das bloße Lesen von Transkriptionen, ohne Nachfrage nach dem Thema des Jazz mit den Ohren (d.h. der Musik zuzuhören) ist ziemlich sinnlos.

Die besten Resultate lassen sich mit diesem Material erzielen, indem die Aufnahmen ausfindig gemacht werden. Selbst wenn sie nicht zu finden sind, so ist schon das Hören anderer Monk-Aufnahmen hilfreich.

Es wird Benutzern dieses Albums auch nahegelegt, die Themen und Akkordsequenzen *auswendig zu lernen*, bevor sie sich an die Soloteile begeben. Es ist nicht nötig, die Soli Note für Note zu spielen, was in jedem Fall auch schwierig sein wird – es sei denn zur Übung. Versuchen Sie stattdessen, Ihre eigenen Soli zu ersetzen. Diese können Teile von Monk enthalten – entweder als direkte Zitate oder Paraphrasen. Die leeren Notensysteme, die bei einigen Stücken vorhanden sind, können Sie dazu verwenden, Ihre eigenen Soloideen niederzuschreiben (mit Bleistift).

Da es interessant ist, zu sehen, wie andere Musiker mit Monks Material improvisieren, enthalten einige der Transkriptionen Soli seiner Mitspieler, wie auch (oder anstelle von) Soli von Monk. Für Holz- und Blechsoli, wie auch für alle Themen, wurden B- und Es-Teile geliefert.

Diskographie der Transkriptionen

Titel, Personen und Aufnahmedaten:

Misterioso, 1947
Monk (Klavier), Milt Jackson (Vibraphon), John Simmons (Bass), Shadow Wilson (Schlagzeug)

'Round About Midnight, 1947
Monk, Sahib Shihab (Altsaxophon), George Taitt (Trompete), Robert Paige (Bass), Art Blakey (Schlagzeug)

Little Rootie Tootie, Hackensack, 15. Oktober 1952
Monk, Gary Mapp (Bass), Art Blakey

Trinkle Trinkle, New York 1957
Monk, John Coltrane (Tenorsaxophon), Wilbur Ware (Bass), Shadow Wilson

Evidence, Five Spot Cafe, New York, August 1958
Monk, Johnny Griffin (Tenorsaxophon), Ahmed Abdul-Malik (Bass), Roy Haynes (Schlagzeug)

Played Twice, New York, Juni 1959
Monk, Thad Jones (Kornett), Charlie Rouse (Tenorsaxophon), Sam Jones (Bass), Art Taylor (Schlagzeug)

Crepuscule with Nellie, Reeves Sound Studios, New York, 26. Juni 1957
Monk, Ray Copeland (Trompete), Gigi Gryce (Altsaxophon), Coleman Hawkins (Tenorsaxophon), Wilbur Ware, Art Blakey.

Vgl.S.5 bezüglich vorhandener Aufzeichnungen

Anmerkungen zu den Transkriptionen

1. MISTERIOSO

Form: 12-taktiger Blues in B♭
Routine: Einleitung 4 Takte; Thema 1 Chorus; Vibraphonsolo 1 Chorus; Klaviersolo 2 Chorusse; Thema 1 Chorus

Das einfache, aber wirkungsvolle Thema von *Misterioso* besteht aus gebrochenen Sexten über einer elementaren Bluessequenz ohne Durchgangsakkorde:

I	IV	I	I
IV	IV	I	I
V	V	I	I

Monk spielt die Melodie während Milt Jackson parallel dazu eine Sexte höher musiziert. Die Melodie in den Takten 1 und 3 (und wieder in den Takten 7 und 8) enthält die große Septe (A) auf dem Tonikaakkord (B). Die erniedrigte Septe (A♭), die man normalerweise über dem Tonikaakkord eines Blues erwarten würde, wird bis Takt 4, wo sie den Wechsel zum E♭7 Akkord im nächsten Takt verstärkt, zurückgehalten. In denselben Takten, in denen Monk die große Septime spielt, trifft Milt Jackson ein Achtel später eine erniedrigte Terz (D♭), was zu einer interessanten Reibung zwischen der erniedrigten Terz ('blue note') und der großen Septe ('non-blue note') führt.

Milt Jacksons lyrisches 12-taktiges Solo verbindet gefühlvolle Bluesstimmung mit langen, fließenden Bebop-Linien. Seine dritte Phrase (Takte 3½ und 4) ist eine Miniaturstudie in der Bop-Stil-Phrasierung, die scheinbar Dizzy Gillespies Einfluß zeigt. Monks spärliche Begleitung reduziert die bereits elementaren Bluesakkorde auf rhythmische Figuren in der Grundstellung, auf die eine Tredezime, die gegen eine erniedrigte Septe gedrängt wird, folgt.

Monks zwei Chorusse (der erste enthält einen zusätzlichen Takt) sind von ungleichmäßiger Verdrehtheit, wogegen Jacksons Solo fast herkömmlich erscheint. Mit einem wiederkehrenden Einfall (1. Chorus, Takte 4-5, 8 und 10-11; 2. Chorus, Takt 8) scheint Monk wie ein Gitarrenspieler Noten zu biegen, indem er die kleinen und großen Terzen zusammen erklingen läßt, dann die große losläßt, während er die kleine festhält.

Zu anderen Einfällen in diesem Solo gehören Phrasen, die zu den erniedrigten Quinten ihrer Akkorde führen (1. Chorus, Takt 2; 2. Chorus, Takte 1-3, Takt 5); und schnelle Läufe, die auf der Ganztonleiter beruhen (1. Chorus, Takte 7, 9; 2. Chorus Takte 4-5, 10-11).

Nach Takt 10 seines ersten Chorus scheint Monk in einem zusätzlichen Takt der Dominante (F7) zu schwelgen, um die absteigenden Figuren in Takt 11 einfügen zu können. Dadurch befindet er sich einen Takt hinter dem Bassisten. Im dritten Takt des nächsten Chorus sind sie jedoch wieder vereint.

Wenn es einen Einwand gegen das *Misterioso*-Thema gibt, dann den gegen seine rhythmische Regelmäßigkeit. Als ob er diesem Einwand vorbeugen wollte, spielte Monk einen wirkungsvollen rhythmischen Kontrapunkt zu Milt Jacksons Linie im letzten Chorus. Er kehrte erste in den letzten Takten zu der ursprünglichen Klavierlinie zurück.

2. 'ROUND ABOUT MIDNIGHT

Form: AABA 32 Takte (8+8+8+8)
Routine: Einleitung 8 Takte, Thema 32 Takte; Solo 8 Takte (+Weiterführung für Schüler 24 Takte; Koda 8 Takte)

Diese berühmteste Jazzballade komponierte Monk offenbar schon in seiner Jugend. Die vorliegende Version beruht auf seiner Blue Note Aufnahme von 1947, jedoch mit den folgenden Änderungen:

1) Die sich überschneidenden Altsaxophon- und Trompetenphrasen der aufgenommenen Einleitung wurden durch eine einzige Oberlinie über dem gespielten Klavierteil ersetzt, Takte 7 und 8 der Einleitung waren ein Kontrabass-*break*.

2) Das vom Klavier gespielte Thema wird so wiedergegeben, wie es gespielt wird; die von der Trompete und dem Saxophon gespielten Harmonieteile wurden jedoch weggelassen. So wie Monk es spielt, verändert sich das Thema bald in eine Paraphrase mit Improvisation. Zum Vergleich wurde eine "durchschnittliche" Version der unverzierten Melodie als oberste Linie über dem Klavierteil hinzugefügt.

3) Die Aufnahme hört mit einem 8-taktigen Klaviersolo nach dem Thema merkwürdig auf. Zu den ersten fünf Takten dieses Solos wurden leere Notensysteme und Akkordsymbole hinzugefügt, um einen vollständigen Chorus für den Studenten zur Fortführung zu haben.

4) Diese Version wird mit der Koda, so, wie sie in verschiedenen, nicht von Monk stammenden Aufnahmen von *Midnight* verwendet wird, abgerundet, z. B. jene von Dizzy Gillespie, Charlie Parker und Miles Davis. (Diese Koda stammt eher von Gillespie als von Monk).

3. LITTLE ROOTIE TOOTIE

Form: AABA 32 Takte (8+8+8+8)
Routine: 3 Takte Einleitung; Thema 32 Takte; Solo 32+16 Takte (1½ Chorusse); Thema 16 Takte (mittlere und letzte 8); Koda 8 Takte

Das Thema von *Little Rootie Tootie* (Monks Sohn gewidmet) ist eine einfallsreiche Entwicklung der idiomatischsten Jazzeinfälle: das Bluesmotiv und Ruf- und Antwort-Muster.

Durch die Umkehrung der letzten beiden Noten (F vor G♭) wird das Anfangsmotiv der 'Ruf'-Phrase als eines der gewöhnlichsten Bluesmotive enthüllt. Auf typisch Monk'sche Art wird die 'Antwort'-Figur mit einer mißtönenden und einzigartigen Dissonanz harmonisiert:

Der *Little Rootie Tootie*-Akkord

D♭○ mit großer und Undezime/
Terz Quarte

Dieser Akkord – nennen wir ihn den *Little Rootie Tootie*-Akkord – *könnte* als verminderter D♭-Akkord mit hinzugefügtem F und G♭ beschrieben werden; für Monk war er jedoch zweifellos nur ein Ton.

In den mittleren 8, durchläuft das ursprüngliche Motiv mit veränderten Intervallen eine Reihe von Transpositionen über "schwierigen" Akkordwechseln, um im letzten Takt auf dem Dominantakkord anzukommen.

Die Haupt-8 des Themas haben keine Akkordsequenz oder Basslinie (in der Aufnahme verdoppelt der Bass die 'Ruf'-Phrase). Die entsprechenden Teile des Solos verwenden jedoch die bekannten 'Rhythmus'-Wechsel (die Version des Jazzmusikers von Gershwins Akkorden *I Got Rhythm*). Während seines Solos führt Monks linke Hand nur ab und zu die Akkorde an; die meiste Zeit sind sie in der Basslinie enthalten. Wenn es Monk paßt, versetzt er den harmonischen Rhythmus. Zum Beispiel im siebten Takt der ersten Mitte-8 erhalten D♭7 und G♭7 je einen Schlag (Schläge 3 und 4) anstelle je eines halben Taktes.

Das Solo, das eines von Monks besten ist (es wurde 1959 von Hall Overton für Monks Town Hall Konzert orchestriert), veranschaulicht deutlich seine Improvisationstaktiken. Im ersten Chorus beginnt jede Haupt-8 mit einer kräftigen, einfachen rhythmischen Phrasierung auf einigen wenigen "offensichtlichen" Noten. Aus diesen Anfängen entwickeln sich die ersten beiden 8 in komplexere, schnellere Phrasierungen. In Takt 5, erste 8, erscheint ein Sechzehntel-Motiv, das später den Höhepunkt des Solos darstellen wird.

Nach dem ersten Chorus fährt das Solo für weitere 16 Takte fort vor der Reprise des Themas der mittleren 8. Die ersten 8 des zweiten Chorus sind eine rhythmische Manipulation der erniedrigten Terz (C♭) und Sext (F) der Tonart, die als mißtönender Tritonus zusammen gespielt werden. In den zweiten 8 wird das Sechzehntel-Halbtonmotiv, das schon vorher in dem Solo vorkam, in 6 Takten verarbeitet. Das Solo endet mit 2 Takten von Sechzehntelfiguren, die durch 4 Oktaven stürzen, um schließlich bei der Mitte-8 Wiederholung anzukommen.

Die letzten 16 Takte dieses Solos symbolisieren für mich das Bild eines überaktiven Arbeiters, der an einem dringenden Projekt im Haus vor sich hin hämmert und bohrt.

4. TRINKLE TRINKLE (in manchen Quellen auch TRINKLE TINKLE)

Form: AABA 30½ Takte (7½+7½+8+7½); Solo Chorusse 32 Takte (8+8+8+8)
Routine: Einleitung (7½ Takte); Thema; Tenorsaxophonsolo; Klaviersolo; Bass-Solo; Thema
Übertragen: Thema (Saxophon- und Klavierteile); Tenorsolo (1. Chorus)

Trinkle Trinkle und *Evidence* (das nächste Stück in diesem Album) stellen die Arbeit von Monks zwei besten Quartetts vor, jenen von 1957/8 mit den Tenorsaxophonisten John Coltrane und Johnny Griffin.

Das *Trinkle*-Thema ist die belebte Kombination einer ursprünglichen Akkordsequenz und einer ungewöhnlichen überaktiven Melodie. Die A-Teile stellen eine komplizierte einleitende Phrase (1½ Takte) einer einfacheren Figur in Takt 3 gegenüber. Im nächsten Takt wird diese Figur nach oben transponiert und nach Takt 5 verlängert, um in Takt 6 zu einer abschließenden Figur zu führen. Die Melodie des A-Teils ist deshalb nur 6 Takte lang. Es folgt ein 1½-Takte langes Schlagzeug *break* anstelle der üblicheren 2-taktigen sich wendenden Bewegung in halbtaktigen Akkorden (I-VI-II-V). Für die Solos erhalten die A-Teile jedoch 8 Takte.

Die mittleren 8 (B-Teil) sind in 4 2-taktige Phrasen unterteilt. Die ersten drei beginnen jeweils mit einer wiederholten Sechzehntel-Figur. Die letzte Phrase, in Vierteln und Achteln, befindet sich absichtlich in den Takten 7-8, und hat eine interessante verminderte Akkordharmonisierung in Takt 7.

John Coltranes Tenorsolo folgt derselben Basslinie wie das Thema. Coltrane interpretiert Takte 3 und 4 des A-Teils jedoch als A♭m7 D♭7/G♭m7 H7 anstelle von A♭7 D♭7/G♭7 H7 wie im Thema. Dieses mächtige Solo ist ein gutes Beispiel für den 'sheets of sound' - Stil, den Coltrane zu jener Zeit kultivierte, und in dem Akkorde in schnell gespielte Skalen erweitert werden.

5. EVIDENCE

Form: AABA 32 Takte
Routine: Einleitung (Klavier) 8 Takte; Thema; Tenorsaxophonsolo; Klaviersolo; Schlagzeugsolo; Thema
Übertragen: Einleitung; Thema (Saxophon- und Klavierteile); Tenorsolo (2. Chorus); Klaviersolo (vollständig)

Im Gegensatz zu *Trinkle Trinkle*, das allein im ersten Takt 17 Noten enthält, ist *Evidence* mit nur 14 Noten, die über die ersten 8 Takte des Themas verteilt sind, sparsamer. Die Mehrzahl dieser Melodienoten sind nur Harmonienoten, eine pro Akkord. Interessant sind die Wahl der Noten und die Art und Weise, mit der die Akkorde versetzt werden, so daß über dem einfachen 4/4 Takt scheinbar ein Kreuztakt suggeriert wird. Die mittleren 8 bestätigen den 4/4 Takt, indem sie einen Akkord/eine Melodienote vor jeden Takt stellen.

Die Melodie von *Evidence ist* demnach die Akkordsequenz, welche wiederum aus den Änderungen des alten *Just You Just Me* stammt. Im folgenden ein Vergleich der ersten 8 von beiden:

Evidence und *Just You Just Me* – Vergleich von Akkordsequenzen Erste, mittlere und letzte 8

EVIDENCE										
:E♭△ / / Gm7	/ / C7 $^{♭5}_{♭9}$ /	/ Fm7 / /	Fm7 B♭7 $^{♭5}_{♭9}$ / /	A7 / / A♭m7	/ D♭7 / /	Fm7	F7 $^{♭5}_{♯9}$
JUST YOU										
:E♭	Gm7* C7	Fm7*	B♭7*	E♭ E♭7	A♭△ A♭m6	F7 B♭7	E♭

FINE

Aus diesem Vergleich läßt sich leicht ersehen, wie sich die ersten 4 Takte von *Evidence* aus den Änderungen von *Just You Just Me* ergeben – durch den Ersatz der mit * gekennzeichneten Akkorde und im Klavierteil durch die Ergänzung von erniedrigten Quinten in den Obernoten zu C7 and B7.

Der zweite Chorus von Johnny Griffins langem Tenorsolo wurde für die Transkription ausgewählt, um zu zeigen, inwiefern ein Improvisator sich dafür entscheiden kann, sich über die scheinbare Komplexität von Monks Änderungen hinwegzusetzen, und stattdessen mit offensichtlichem Humor über den einfacheren Änderungen, von denen die Monk'schen stammen, spielt.

6. PLAYED TWICE

Form: AABA (4+4+4+4) wiederholt
Routine: Thema; Kornettsolo; Tenorsaxophonsolo; Klaviersolo; Thema
Übertragen: Thema (Melodielinie und Klavierteile); Kornettsolo (1. Chorus)

Dieses wiederholte 16-taktige Thema kann als komprimierte AABA-Form beschrieben werden, eher in 4- als in 8-taktigen Teilen. Es ist eine zufriedenstellende Komposition Monks mit einer eng argumentierten motivischen Entwicklung und einer merkwürdigen aber nicht komplexen Akkordsequenz.

15

Das ganze Thema entwickelt sich aus den Weiterführungen der einleitenden Figur. Wir nennen diese Figur und ihre Weiterführung (a) und (b):

(a) Figur (b) Fortsetzung

Figur (a) in 3/8 Gegenrhythmus wird durch eine gewöhnliche Bewegung harmonisiert C∆ zu D♭7. D♭7 ertönt auf dem 4. Schlag von Takt 1 und wird in den Takten 2 und 3 weitergeführt als Harmonie zu Figur (b). Die letzten beiden Noten dieser Figur werden in Takt 4 wiederholt, jedoch einen Schlag später und auf einen unerwarteten Akkord, A13, transponiert. Als ob die Musik mit dieser Lösung unzufrieden ist, versucht sie es wieder. Dieses Mal (in Takt 7) werden die letzten beiden Noten von Figur (b) nicht wiederholt, sondern sofort auf einen neuen Akkord transponiert, Gm9, der zwei Takte anhält. Ist das genug? Scheinbar nicht. Als neue Taktik wird Figur (b) auf einen anderen neuen Akkord transponiert, eine besondere Monk'sche Intonation von F7 mit B darüber. Über vier Takten dieses Akkords wird Figur (b) dreimal gespielt, in 5-schlägigen Abständen, kommt aber immer noch nicht zur Ruhe. In einem letzten Versuch fängt die Musik wieder am Anfang an. Dieses Mal dehnt sich Figur (b) aus, um einen Weg von D♭7 über Gm7 und A13 zu finden, um schließlich auf D∆ zu enden. Der unerwartete A13 Akkord in Takt 4 signalisierte vielleicht diese mögliche Lösung. Jetzt stellt sich aber die Frage: Steht das Stück in C oder D? Wir können uns vorstellen, was Monk von solchen Fragen gehalten hätte . . .

7. CREPUSCULE WITH NELLIE

Beim letzten Stück in unserer einleitenden Sammlung von Werken Monks – einer seiner hervorragendsten Balladen – geben wir einen Instrumentalteil wieder. Wenn man weiß, daß "crepuscule" aus dem Lateinischen kommt und "Dämmerung" bedeutet und daß mit Nellie natürlich Monks Frau gemeint ist, läßt sich sowohl aus dem Titel als auch der Stimmung des Stücks schließen, daß es eine besondere, gemeinsame Zeit behandelt.

Anstelle einer vollständig ergänzten Klavierfassung geben wir nur die Melodie und die Akkordsymbole wieder – eine ideale Gelegenheit für Pianisten, Gitarristen und schließlich auch Bearbeiter, ihr Wissen von Monks Akkordstil mit den Symbolen zu realisieren. Nachdem Sie dieses ausprobiert haben, könnten Sie einen anderen Stil für die Textur verwenden, zum Beispiel jenen von Bill Evans, (der, wie bekannt ist, Monk tiefen Respekt entgegenbrachte. Evans Fassungen von *'Round Midnight** sind ausgezeichnete Beispiele dafür, wie ein anderer Stilist Monk interpretiert. Man erzählt sich übrigens, daß Evans am Anfang seiner Karriere in New York gelegentlich nachts in Monks Wohnung übernachtete und Monk die ganze Nacht für seinen Besucher musizierte . . .).

*auf den Alben *Trio 64* und *Conversation with Myself* von Bill Evans

Avant-Propos

Après Charlie Parker et Louis Armstrong, Thelonious Monk est la troisième figure de jazz à être le sujet d'une étude par Novello. La compilation de ces albums a été une expérience instructive. M'étant tourné vers Armstrong après l'album sur Parker, je m'attendais à une tâche plus aisée. J'avais tort: le phrasé rythmique d'Armstrong s'est avéré difficile à transcrire. J'ai appris ma leçon: ne pas considérer le jazz "traditionnel" comme allant de soi.

Tous ceux qui connaissent la musique de Monk savent très bien qu'elle est difficilement transcrivible. Les transcriptions dans cet album sont aussi justes que possible, mais d'autres oreilles n'auraient pas tort d'entendre certains détails différemment. Ce que j'ai surtout retenu de cet exercice, c'est une meilleure appréciation de l'originalité et de l'intégrité réelles de Monk comme compositeur et improvisateur de jazz. Son originalité semble être du meilleur cru, qui a mûri d'une solide connaissance de la tradition du jazz, à commencer par le blues.

Si cet album encourage une appréciation plus large des qualités uniques de Monk, il aura valu la peine d'avoir été compilé. LIONEL GRIGSON

Biographie Sommaire

Thelonious Monk naquit le 10 octobre 1920 à Rocky Mount, en Caroline du Nord. Ses parents s'appelaient Thelonious (Senior) et Barbara Monk. Nous supposons ainsi que ce prénom peu commun transmis de père en fils fut d'abord choisi par les grands-parents paternels du fils. Son deuxième prénom, tout aussi inhabituel, Sphere, était celui du grand-père maternel de son père.

Dans les années 20, Monk s'installa avec sa famille à New York. Là, il bénéficia de cours privés de piano, même s'il semble l'avoir principalement appris tout seul. Dès l'âge de 15 ans il travaillait déjà comme pianiste, tout en étudiant dans un lycée. C'est alors qu'il rencontra un batteur qui deviendrait un collègue important, Kenny Clarke. A ce moment-là, ou un peu plus tard, Monk accompagna un groupe de négro-spiritual pendant un temps. C'est aussi lors de son adolescence que Monk fut associé avec le remarquable trompettiste Cootie Williams, pour lequel – ou avec lequel – il composa 'Round About Midnight.

Dès les années 40, Monk travaillait comme pianiste régulier dans le Minton's Club à New York. C'est là qu'avec Charlie Parker, Dizzie Gillespie et Kenny Clarke, Monk fit partie du petit noyau de musiciens reconnus pour avoir developpé le "jazz moderne".

A cette époque, bien que Monk fût toujours inconnu du public de jazz, son travail était manifestement intéressant pour ses collègues musiciens. Il était apprecié non seulement par les jeunes "modernistes" mais aussi par les artistes "swing" plus avancés des années 30, y compris les stars du saxophone ténor Coleman Hawkins et Ben Webster. Ces deux derniers allaient régulièrement au Minton's pour assister aux spectacles, avec l'intention manifeste d'apprendre les accords et les mélodies de Monk. En 1944, Monk eut son premier contact important avec le grand public quand Hawkins l'embaucha pour un emploi régulier au 52nd Street et enregistra un disque avec lui. Néanmoins il y eut peu de travail pour Monk jusqu'aux années 50, même s'il commença à enregistrer pour Blue Note en 1947.

Le début des années 50 auraient pu voir la percée de Monk si, en 1951, il n'avait pas été banni des clubs de New York à la suite d'une affaire de drogue mineure qui l'avait empêché d'y travailler. A partir des années 1952-55, Monk enregistra pour Prestige, et en 1956, l'album *Brilliant Corners* chez Riverside accueillit de bonnes critiques.

Lorsqu'il recouvra le droit de jouer à New York en 1957, Monk fut pris dans le club Five Spot de New York, pour un contrat prolongé dans deux excellents quartettes avec les saxophonistes ténor John Coltrane (1957) et Johnny Griffin (1958). Ce contrat, ainsi que des ventes de disques montantes, lui servit de tremplin pour un succès constant et des aventures telles que l'excellent orchestre de 10 instruments de 1959. Pendant le reste de sa carrière de musicien, Monk joua la plupart du temps dans le quartette avec le saxophoniste ténor Charlie Rouse. Bien que Rouse ait été un interprète digne des compositions de Monk, ce quartette n'atteindra jamais les sommets des quartettes de Coltrane et Griffin.

Monk avait la cinquantaine bien tassée quand il quitta sa femme de plusieurs années, Nellie, et devint le compagnon d'une autre admiratrice de longue date, la Baronne Nica de Königswater, sans qu'il y eût jamais d'animosité entre les deux femmes. A la fin de sa vie, Monk paraît avoir perdu tout intérêt pour le piano. Il mourut à Englewood, dans le New Jersey, le 17 février 1982, âgé de 61 ans.

Le Style de Thelonious Monk

Bien qu'on mentionne toujours Monk aux côtés de Charlie Parker et de Dizzie Gillespie comme l'un des fondateurs du jazz moderne, son style mélodique et rythmique n'a rien du style soi-disant "bop" des ses collègues. Leur point commun est leur approche de l'harmonie.

Pour leur servir de support de fond pour leurs solos qui se chevauchaient, Parker et Gillespie aimaient entendre des grilles d'accords qui, bien qu'inspirées de chansons classiques, étaient renforcées par l'utilisation d'arrangements de voix divers, de notes ajoutées, d'accords de passage et de substitution. De telles possibilités ont été explorées à fond par Art Tatum dans les années 30. Monk semble avoir emprunté et codifié l'approche harmonique de Tatum et en avoir passé les principes aux boppeurs. Vous trouverez ci-dessous quelques exemples de la façon dont une progression II-V-I peut être réorganisée et substituée à la manière de Monk:

(a) Accord classique (à eviter)   (b) Accord "allégé"

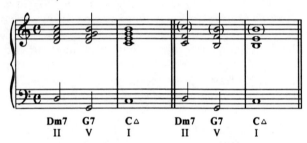

(c) Addition d'une quinte bémol à l'accord de V^e degré (mouvement contraire à la main droite).

(d) Addition d'une quinte bémol aux accords de IIe et V^e degrés.

(e) L'accord de V^e degré avec sa quinte bémol à la basse devient un accord de IIe degré.

(f) L'accord de IIe degré avec sa quinte bémol à la basse devient un accord de VIe degré.

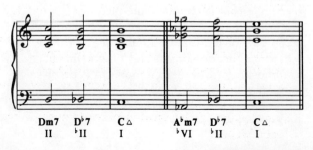

La composition *Evidence* de Monk dans cet album montre comment une structure harmonique/mélodique intéressante et inhabituelle peut être développée à partir d'une grille de base simple en ajoutant des quintes bémol et en déplaçant le rythme harmonique (cf. les Notes sur les Transcriptions p.22).

Les accords de Monk, ainsi qu'il les a décrits lui-même sont parfaitement logiques. Mais entre ses mains la logique de l'arrangement des voix et de la substitution résulte en un style d'harmonie individuel dont la caractéristique principale est une amertume apparemment voulue.

La musique de Monk est empreinte d'un puissant sens de développement mélodique et rythmique qui, dans une large mesure, pourrait fonctionner indépendamment de l'harmonie. Monk travaille souvent par un processus de répétition et de déplacement d'idées les plus simples, essentiellement des motifs de blues, qui entraîne une asymétrie satisfaisante. Ceci est bien illustré dans la phrase de Blues *Straight No Chaser* de Monk, qui est un développement d'un motif ou point initial unique:

motif de blues: *Straight No Chaser*

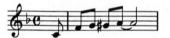

Développement asymétrique du motif: *Straight No Chaser*

On peut diviser le thème de *Straight No Chaser* en 4 phrases notées ci-dessous (a), (b), (c) et (d), les 2 premières étant de la même longueur, la 3ème plus courte et la dernière la plus longue.

La phrase (a) enchaîne le motif initial et une répétition, et finit avec deux notes supplémentaires.

La phrase (b) commence avec le même motif avancé d'un temps dans la mesure. Ce motif est répété deux fois sans pauses: la deuxième reprise est amputée d'une note pour arriver sur le premier temps de la 5ème mesure.

La phrase (c) reprend le même motif comme il est répété et allongé en (a), mais ici il est isolé et a une nouvelle position dans la mesure.

La phrase (d) commence comme si elle récapitulait (b). Cette fois-ci, la deuxième reprise du motif n'est pas raccourcie mais au contraire allongée d'une "queue" de 12 notes qui amène à une dernière exposition du motif.

LE PROBLEME DE LA FORME:
LA SOLUTION DE MONK

Les performances de jazz consistent d'habitude en des solos improvisés sur une grille d'accords répétée, avec un thème joué au début et à la fin. Ce format pratique peut aboutir à de la grande musique entre les mains de solistes inspirés. Mais on peut objecter que le résultat final ne donne pas une forme d'ensemble satisfaisante. En même temps on a souvent étouffé la musique en essayant d'imposer cette forme en plaçant le jazz dans une structure composée ou arrangée. Comme Jelly Roll Morton et Duke Ellington, Thelonious Monk est l'un des rares compositeurs à avoir combiné composition et improvisation de sorte qu'elles se mettent respectivement en valeur.

Monk savait bien que ses solistes étaient à l'aise avec une forme strophique de grilles d'accords répétée, et il ne changeait pas cette routine pour ne pas interrompre le cours de leur interprétation. Sa solution instinctive pour le problème de la forme était non seulement de composer des thèmes intéressants mais aussi de créer ses propres improvisations à partir de leurs mélodies et de leurs rythmes et pas seulement de leurs accords. C'est-à-dire que Monk improvise autant sur la mélodie que sur la grille d'accords. Ses accompagnements montrent le même souci d'unification. Plutôt que de n'être que des accords placés "sur le rythme", ils sont une sorte de récapitulation constamment renouvelée du thème. Dans ses meilleures compositions (par exemple *Evidence*, dans cet album), cette approche donne à la performance une sensation de mouvement constant d'expansion puis retour aux origines thématiques.

Transcriptions et Mode d'Emploi

Il faut aborder les transcriptions de jazz avec prudence. L'aptitude à déchiffrer la musique et celle à improviser dans un style jazz ne s'excluent pas, mais sont des modes d'activité musicale différents qui requièrent des savoir-faire différents. Il ne sert à rien de lire des transcriptions si on ne fait pas de recherches auditives (autrement dit, si on n'écoute pas la musique) dans le domaine du jazz.

Les meilleurs résultats à partir de ce matériel seront obtenus en écoutant systématiquement les enregistrements correspondants. Et même si vous ne pouvez pas les trouver, il vous sera toujours utile d'écouter un enregistrement quelconque de Monk.

Les utilisateurs de cet album sont fortement conseillés de *mémoriser* les thèmes et les grilles d'accord avant de travailler sur les parties de solos. A moins de s'en servir comme exercice, il n'est pas besoin de jouer les solos note pour note — ce qui, de toutes façons, ne sera pas chose aisée. Visez plutôt à leur substituer vos propres solos. Ces derniers peuvent être inspirés de compositions de Monk ou en reproduire certaines partiellement. Les portées de continuation vierges que l'on trouve dans quelques morceaux peuvent être utilisées pour y annoter au crayon vos propres idées de solo.

Comme il est intéressant de voir comment d'autres musiciens improvisent sur des compositions de Monk, certaines transcriptions comprennent des solos de ses acolytes ainsi que (ou au lieu de) ceux de Monk. Pour les solos d'instruments à hanche et de cuivres, ainsi que pour tous les thèmes, on a fourni des parties en Si bémol et en Mi bémol.

Discographie des Transcriptions

Titres, noms des musiciens et dates d'enregistrement:

Misterioso, 1947
Monk (piano), Milt Jackson (vibraphone), John Simmons (basse), Shadow Wilson (batterie)

'Round About Midnight, 1947
Monk, Sahib Shihab (saxophone alto), George Taitt (trompette), Robert Paige (basse), Art Blakey (batterie)

Little Rootie Tootie, Hackensack, 15 octobre 1952
Monk, Gary Mapp (basse), Art Blakey

Trinkle Trinkle, New York, 1957
Monk, John Coltrane (saxophone ténor), Wilbur Ware (basse), Shadow Wilson

Evidence, Five Spot Cafe, New York, août 1958
Monk, Johnny Griffin (saxophone ténor), Ahmed Abdul-Malik, Roy Haynes (batterie)

Played Twice, New York, juin 1959
Monk, Thad Jones (cornet), Charlie Rouse (saxophone ténor), Sam Jones (basse), Art Taylor (batterie)

Crepuscule with Nellie, Reeves Sound Studios, New York, 26 juin 1957
Monk, Ray Copeland (trompette), Gigi Gryce (saxophone alto), Coleman Hawkins (saxophone ténor), Wilbur Ware, Art Blakey.

Pour la disponibilité des enregistrements voir p.5

Notes sur les Transcriptions

1. MISTERIOSO

Forme: blues de 12 mesures en B♭
Procédure: 4 mesures d'introduction; thème, 1 chorus; solo vibraphone, 1 chorus; solo piano, 2 chorus; thème, 1 chorus.

Le thème simple mais efficace de *Misterioso* est construit à partir de sixtes arpégées sur une grille de blues de base sans les accords de passage:

I	IV	I	I
IV	IV	I	I
V	V	I	I

Monk s'occupe de la mélodie pendant que Milt Jackson joue en parallèle une sixte au-dessus. Aux mesures 1 et 3, ainsi qu'aux mesures 7 et 8 de la mélodie, on trouve une 7ème majeure (A) sur un accord de tonique (B♭). La 7ème bémol (A♭) que l'on attendrait avec un accord de tonique en blues, n'arrive qu'à la mesure 4, où elle renforce le changement pour l'accord de E♭7 de la mesure d'après. Aux mesures où Monk joue une 7ème majeure, Milt Jackson attaque une tierce bémol (D♭) une croche plus tard, créant une dissonance intéressante entre une note qui n'est pas une "blue note" (la 7ème majeure) et la tierce bémol qui en est une.

Le solo lyrique de 12 mesures de Milt Jackson combine des inflexions de blues sentimal avec des phrases "bop" longues et fluides. Sa troisième phrase, aux mesures 3½ et 4, est une étude en miniature qui fait penser au phrasé style "bop", semblant refléter l'influence de Dizzie Gillespie. L'accompagnement sobre de Monk réduit les accords de blues déjà de base à des figures rythmiques de fondamentale suivies de 13ème plaquée contre 7ème bémol.

Les 2 chorus de Monk -le premier comprenant une mesure supplémentaire – ont une perversité irrégulière qui font paraître le solo de Jackson presque conventionnel. Monk, en utilisant un procédé récurrent (1er chorus, mesures 4-5, 8 et 10-11; 2nd chorus, mesure 8) semble "tordre" ses notes comme un guitariste, en faisant sonner les tierces mineures et majeures ensemble et en relâchant ensuite la tierce majeure tout en tenant la mineure.

D'autres procédés sont utilisés dans ce solo comme des phrases se terminant sur les quintes bémol de leurs accords (1er chorus, 2ème mesure; 2nd chorus, mesures 1-3, 5ème mesure) ou des roulades rapides sur gamme tonale (1er chorus, mesures 7 et 9; 2nd chorus, mesures 4-5, 10-11).

Après la 10ème mesure de son premier chorus, Monk semble se laisser aller à jouer une mesure supplémentaire de la dominante (F7), de façon à inclure les groupes de notes descendantes à la 11ème mesure. Ce qui lui donne une mesure de retard sur le bassiste, mais ils sont de nouveau ensemble dès la 3ème mesure du chorus suivant.

Si l'on peut faire quelque objection sur le thème de *Misterioso*, c'est à propos de sa régularité rythmique. Mais, comme s'il avait prévu cette critique, Monk joue un contrepoint rythmique efficace à la phrase de Milt Jackson dans le dernier chorus, ne retournant à sa partition de piano d'origine que pour les dernières mesures.

2. 'ROUND ABOUT MIDNIGHT

Forme: AABA 32 mesures (8+8+8+8)
Procédure: 8 mesures d'introduction; thème, 32 mesures; solo, 8 mesures (+24 de continuation pour l'étudiant); coda, 8 mesures.

C'est la plus célèbre de toutes les ballades de jazz. Monk l'a apparemment composée alors qu'il était encore adolescent. La version que nous donnons ici est celle de l'enregistrement de 1947 chez Blue Note, mais avec les modifications suivantes:

1) Dans l'introduction, on a remplacé les phrases du saxophone alto et de la trompette qui se chevauchaient par une seule voix dans les aigus, qui est écrite au-dessus de la partition du piano. Aux mesures 7 et 8 de l'introduction il y avait un break de la contrebasse.

2) Le thème, joué par le piano, est donné tel quel, mais les parties harmoniques jouées par la trompette et le saxophone ont été omises. Le thème, tel que Monk le jouait, devient très vite une paraphrase/improvisation. Nous avons ajouté, en guise de comparaison, une version "moyenne" de la mélodie toute seule au-dessus de la partie du piano.

3) Bizarrement, l'enregistrement finit par un solo de 8 mesures au piano après le thème. Des portées vides et des noms d'accords ont été ajoutés aux 5 premières mesures de ce solo pour que l'étudiant puisse continuer le chorus.

4. Cette version s'achève avec une coda qui a été utilisée dans de nombreux enregistrements de *Midnight* par d'autres musiciens que Monk, tels que Dizzie Gillespie, Charlie Parker et Miles Davies (il est possible que ce soit Gillespie qui en soit à l'origine, plutôt que Monk).

3. LITTLE ROOTIE TOOTIE

Forme: AABA 32 mesures (8+8+8+8)
Procédure: 3 mesures d'introduction; thème, 32 mesures; solo, 32+16 (1½ chorus); thème, 16 ("middle" et "last" 8); coda, 8.

Le thème de *Little Rootie Tootie*, que Monk a dédié à son fils, est le développement original des procédés de jazz les plus idiomatiques: le motif de blues et le modèle de "question-réponse".

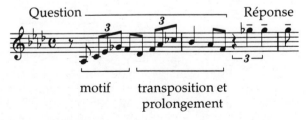

Le motif initial de "question" est révélé comme l'un des motifs de blues les plus ordinaires de tous, avec les deux notes renversées de la fin (F avant G♭). Mais la "réponse", dans un procédé typiquement Monk, est jouée en harmonie avec une dissonance unique:

L'accord *Little Rootie Tootie*

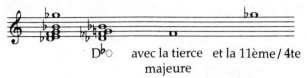

D♭○ avec la tierce   et la 11ème / 4te
majeure

Cet accord – appelons-le l'accord *Little Rootie Tootie* – pourrait être décrit comme un accord de D♭ diminué ajouté d'un F et d'un G♭, mais pour Monk ce devait sûrement n'être qu'un son.

Dans le "middle 8", lors de changements d'accord "difficiles", le motif original avec intervalles changés est amené à une série de transpositions pour arriver à un accord de dominante sur le dernier temps.

Les "main 8s" (c'est-à-dire les parties A) du thème n'ont ni grille d'accords ni ligne de basse (dans l'enregistrement, la basse double la "question"). Mais les parties de solo correspondantes utilisent les changements "rhythmiques" familiers (la version du musicien de jazz des accords de *I Got Rhythm* de Gershwin). Pendant ce solo, la main gauche de Monk ne joue les accords que de temps en temps, la plupart du temps ils sont implicitement présents dans la ligne de basse. Lorsque cela l'arrange, Monk déplace le rythme harmonique. Par exemple, à la 7ème mesure du premier "middle 8", il tient D♭7 et G♭7 une noire chacun (noires 3 et 4) au lieu d'une demi-mesure chacun.

Le solo de Monk, qui compte parmi ses meilleurs (Hall Overton le lui orchestra pour son concert de 1959 au Town Hall), illustre parfaitement ses tactiques d'improvisation. Dans le premier chorus, toutes les "main 8" commencent par un phrasé rythmique puissant et simple sur seulement quelques notes "évidentes". A partir de ce début, les 2 premières séries de 8 mesures se développent en un phrasé plus complexe et rapide. A la 5ème mesure du "first 8", un motif de double croche apparaît qui formera plus tard le point culminant du solo.

Après le premier chorus, le solo continue pendant encore 16 mesures avant la reprise du thème à partir du "middle 8". Le "first 8" du 2nd chorus est une manipulation rythmique de la tierce bémol (C♭) et de la sixte (F) de la clé, jouées ensemble pour un effet de triton discordant. Dans le "second 8" le motif double croche-demi-ton du début du solo est travaillé pendant 6 mesures. Le solo finit par 2 mesures de double croches qui descendent depuis 4 octaves pour arriver à la reprise du "middle 8".

Les 16 dernières mesures du solo créent dans mon esprit l'image d'un ouvrier hyperactif, affairé à quelque tâche domestique, avec son marteau et sa perceuse.

4. TRINKLE TRINKLE (ou TRINKLE TINKLE selon d'autres sources)

Forme: AABA 30½ mesures (7½+7½+8+7½); chorus en solos, 32 mesures (8+8+8+8)
Procédure: introduction, 7½ mesures; thème; solo saxophone ténor; solo piano; solo basse; thème.
Transcription: thème (parties du saxophone et du piano); solo ténor (1er chorus).

Trinkle Trinkle et *Evidence* (le morceau qui suit dans cet album) représentent le travail des 2 meilleurs quartettes de Monk, celui de 1957-8 avec les saxophonistes ténor John Coltrane et Johnny Griffin.

Le thème de *Trinkle Trinkle* est une combinaison exaltante d'une grille d'accords originale et d'une mélodie inhabituelle hyperactive. Les parties A comprennent une phrase d'ouverture complexe (1½ mesures) contrastant avec une phrase plus simple à la mesure 3. A la mesure suivante, cette dernière est transposée au-dessus et jouée jusqu'à la 5ème mesure pour se terminer à la 6ème mesure. Par conséquent la mélodie de la partie A ne dure que 6 mesures. Elle est suivie d'un break d'une mesure et demie à la batterie au lieu d'un mouvement plus habituel de retour en arrière en 2 mesures réalisé en 2 accords par mesure (I-VI-II-V). Mais les parties A deviennent des parties de 8 mesures pour les solos.

La partie B, "middle 8", est divisée en 4 phrases de 4 mesures; les 3 premières commençant chacune par un motif double croche répété. La dernière phrase, en croches et noires est volontairement repoussée aux mesures 7-8, et comprend une harmonisation d'accords diminués intéressante à la 7ème mesure.

Le solo de John Coltrane suit la même ligne de basse que celle du thème. Cependant, aux mesures 3 et 4 de la partie A, Coltrane joue A♭m7 D♭7 / G♭m7 B7 plutôt que A♭7 D♭7 / G♭7 B7, comme pour le thème. Ce puissant solo est une bonne illustration du style "mur de son" que Coltrane utilisait à cette époque, les accords étant développés en gammes éxécutées rapidement.

5. EVIDENCE

Forme: AABA 32 mesures
Procédure: 8 mesures d'introduction au piano; thème; solo saxophone ténor; solo piano; solo batterie; thème.
Transcription: introduction; thème (parties du saxophone et du piano); solo ténor (2nd chorus); solo piano (en entier).

Contrairement à *Trinkle Trinkle*, qui contenait 17 notes rien que dans la première mesure, *Evidence* est économique, n'en contenant que 14 pour les 8 premières mesures du thème. La plupart de ces notes de mélodie ne sont que des notes d'harmonie, une par accord, ce qui est intéressant est le choix de ces notes, et la manière dont les accords sont déplacés de sorte qu'ils suggèrent un 3/4 sur un 4/4 tout simple. Le "middle 8" réaffirme le 4/4 en plaçant une note d'accord/de mélodie juste avant chaque mesure.

La mélodie d'*Evidence* "est", par conséquent, la grille d'accords. Elle s'avère dérivée d'adaptations du vieux classique *Just You Just Me*, les accords notés * ayant été déplacés et, dans la partie du piano, les notes de quinte bémol du dessus ayant été ajoutées à C7 et B♭7.

Evidence et *Just You Just Me* – Comparaison des grilles d'accord: First, second & last 8

EVIDENCE :E♭△ / / Gm7	♭5 ♭9 / / C7 /	/ Fm7 / /	♭5 ♭9 Fm7 B♭7 / /	A7 / / A♭m7	/ D♭7 / /	Fm7	♭5 ♯9 F7 FINE
JUST YOU : E♭	* Gm7 C7	* Fm7	* B♭7	E♭ E♭7	A♭△ A♭m6	F7 B♭7	E♭

Nous avons décidé de transcrire le second chorus du long solo ténor de Johnny Griffin pour montrer comment un improvisateur peut choisir de surmonter l'apparente complexité des changements de Monk, et de jouer à la place, avec un sens de l'humour évident, des changements plus simples dont ceux de Monk sont dérivés.

6. PLAYED TWICE

Forme: AABA (4+4+4+4) répété
Procédure: thème; solo cornet; solo saxophone ténor; solo piano; thème.
Transcription: thème (parties des solistes et du piano); solo cornet (1er chorus).

Ce thème de 16 mesures répété peut être décrit comme une forme AABA comprimée, en 4 mesures plutôt qu'en 8. C'est une composition de Monk satisfaisante comprenant un développement du motif solidement argumenté et une grille d'accords étrange mais non complexe.

Le thème entier est dérivé des suites de la phrase d'ouverture. Nous appellerons cette phrase et sa suite respectivement (a) et (b):

(a) motif   (b) prolongement

La phrase (a), dans un rythme syncopé 3/8 est harmonisée par un mouvement habituel C△/D♭7. D♭7 arrive sur le 4ème temps de la 1ère mesure, et est tenu jusqu' aux mesures 2 et 3 comme harmonie de la phrase (b). Les 2 dernières notes de cette phrase sont répétées à la 4ème mesure, mais un temps plus tard et transposées dans un accord inhabituel, A13. Comme si cette conclusion était insatisfaisante, une autre solution est essayée. Cette fois (à la 7ème mesure), les 2 dernières notes de la phrase (b) ne sont pas répétées mais immédiatement transposées dans un nouvel accord, Gm9, qui dure 2 mesures. Cela conviendra-t-il? Apparement non, puisque, dans une nouvelle tactique, la phrase (b) est transposée dans un autre accord, Monk juxtaposant B♭ à F7. La phrase (b) est jouée 3 fois sur plus de 4 mesures de cet accord, à des intervalles de 5 temps, mais cette tactique n'aboutit toujours pas. Dans un ultime effort, la musique recommence depuis le début. Cette fois-ci, la phrase s'allonge pour cheminer de D♭7 jusqu'à Gm7 et A13 pour finir tranquillement sur D△. Il est possible que l'accord inattendu de A13 de la 4ème mesure ait annoncé cette conclusion. Mais maintenant se pose la question de savoir si ce morceau est en C ou en D? On peut deviner ce que Monk aurait pensé d'une telle question ...

7. CREPUSCULE WITH NELLIE

La dernière partition sur encart de notre collection sur Monk concerne l'une des ballades les plus remarquables qu'il ait écrites. Si vous vous souvenez que Nellie était sa femme, vous pouvez deviner d'après le choix du titre et l'humeur du morceau qu'il décrit un moment privilégié qu'ils ont partagés (le mot "crepuscule", en anglais, qui est beaucoup moins courant que son équivalent germanique "twilight", donne un effet comique).

Nous avons préféré fournir uniquement la mélodie et les noms d'accords, plutôt qu'une version "tout piano" donnant ainsi la possibilité aux pianistes, guitaristes, et arrangeurs d'ailleurs, d'appliquer leur connaissance du style d'accords qu'utilise Monk à l'interprétation de ce morceau. Ceci fait, il est possible d'adopter un style différent, celui de Bill Evans, par exemple. (Celui-ci avait, bien sûr, un profond respect pour Monk. Les versions que Evans a exécutées de 'Round Midnight* illustrent parfaitement la façon dont un autre musicien peut résoudre le problème d'interprétation d'une composition de Monk. J'ajoute qu'à ses débuts à New York, il paraît qu'il passait quelquefois la nuit chez Monk et celui-ci jouait pour lui pendant toute la nuit . . .).

*Versions des albums Trio 64 et Conversations with Myself de Bill Evans.

1. MISTERIOSO

N.B. quavers in intro. and theme are played as written; i.e. not swung.

© Copyright 1979 Bocu Music Ltd.

25

1st Chorus

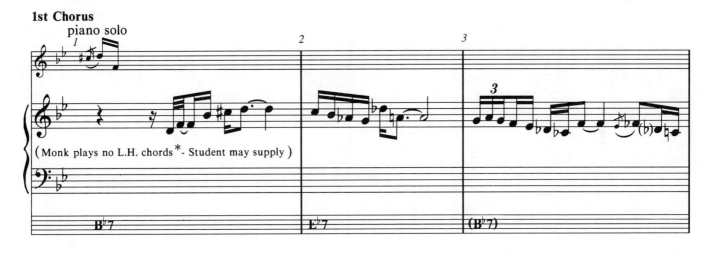

(Monk plays no L.H. chords* - Student may supply)

* except in bar 9, 2nd Chorus.

2. 'ROUND ABOUT MIDNIGHT

Thelonious Monk and Cootie Williams

3. LITTLE ROOTIE TOOTIE

© Copyright 1979 Bocu Music Ltd.

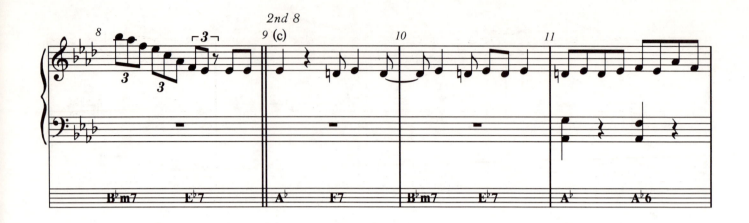

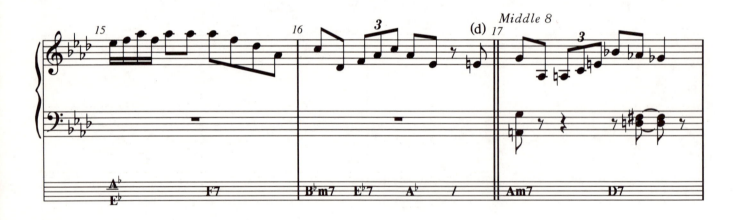
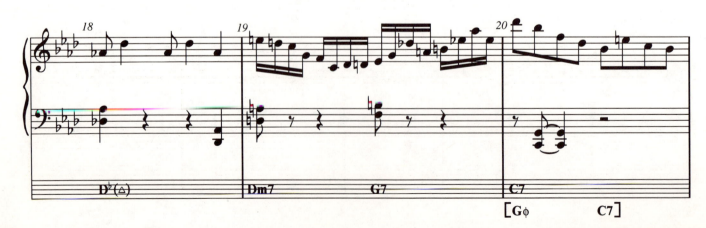

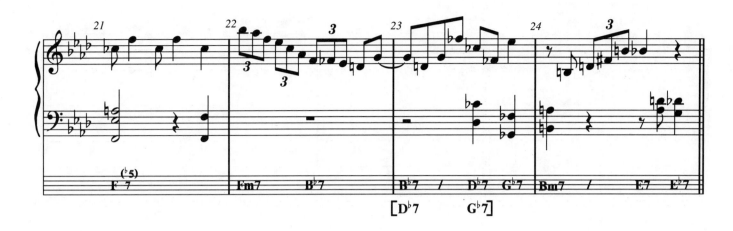
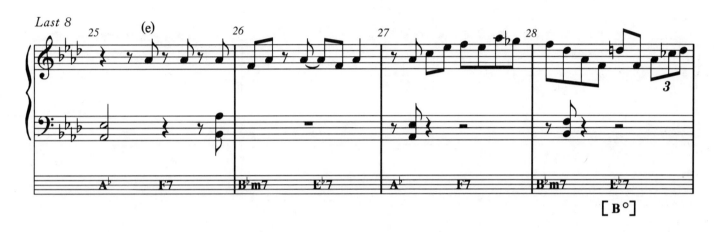
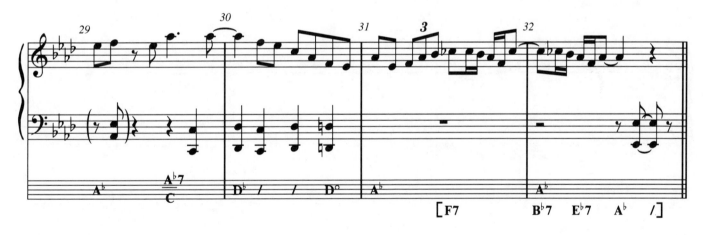

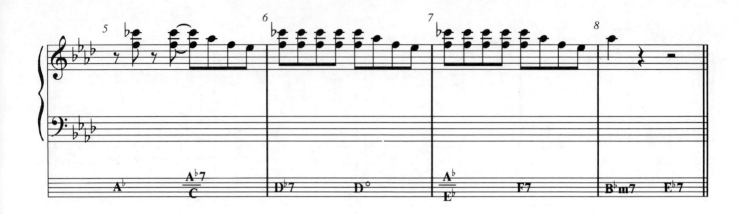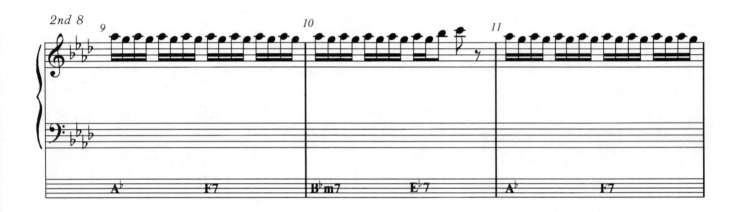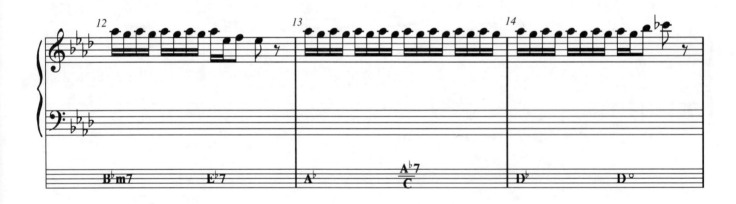

CODA

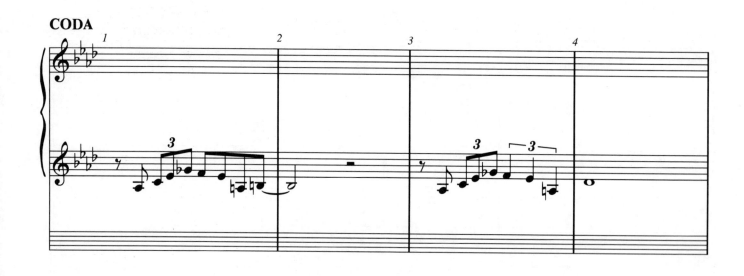

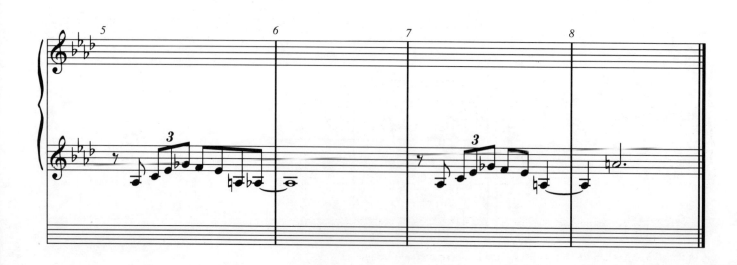

4. TRINKLE TRINKLE

* In the quartet version, the bracketed section is played by tenor saxophone.

© Copyright 1979 Bocu Music Ltd.

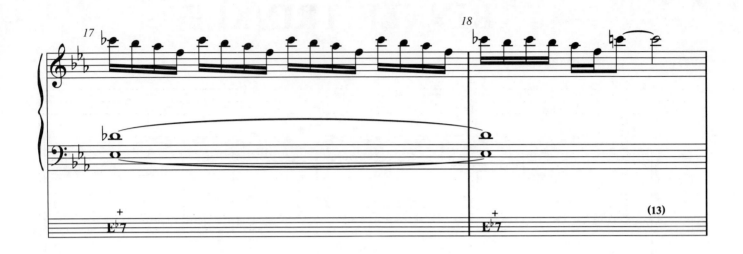
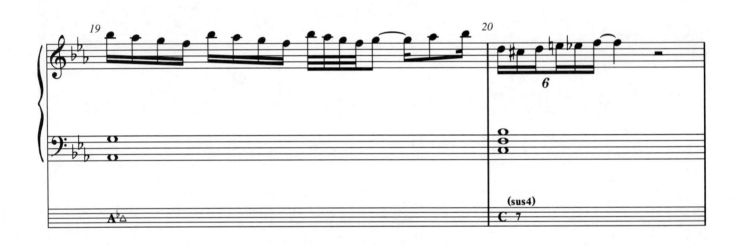

D.C. (3) then to solos. Last Chorus: D.C. al ⊕

5. EVIDENCE

Bright medium tempo ♩= c.170

© Copyright 1979 Bocu Music Ltd.

CHORDS FOR SAMPLE SOLO (see separate lead parts)

* Solo line implies A♭△ rather than A♭m7 as in theme

Piano solo (2 choruses)

1st Chorus *1st 8*

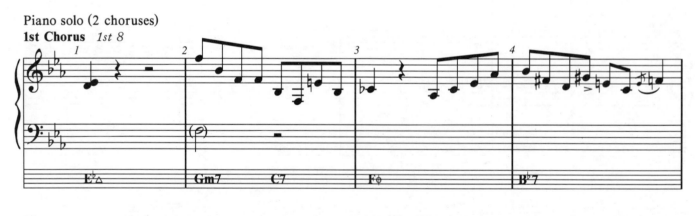

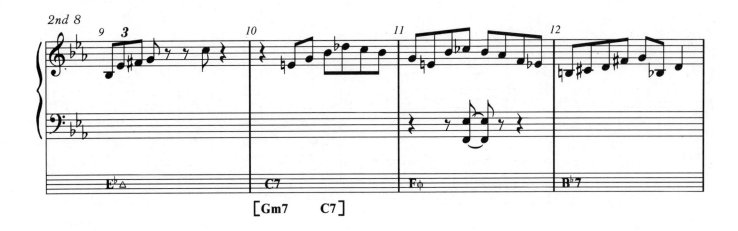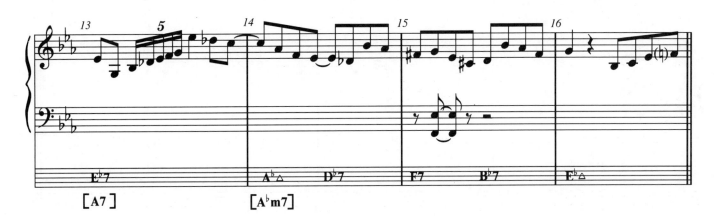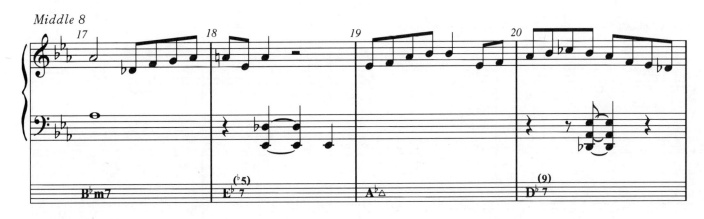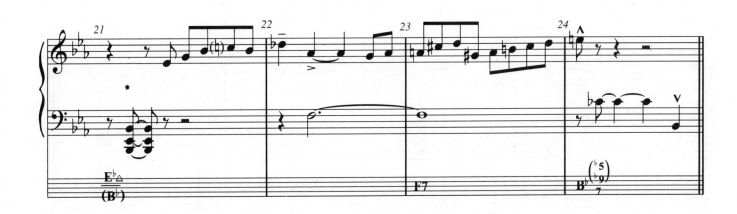

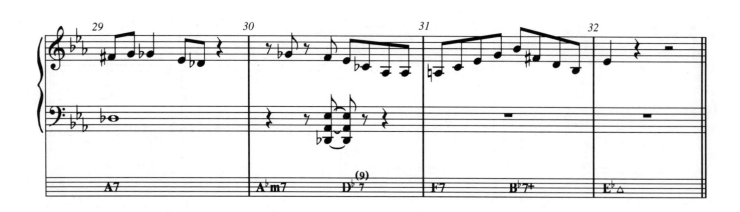
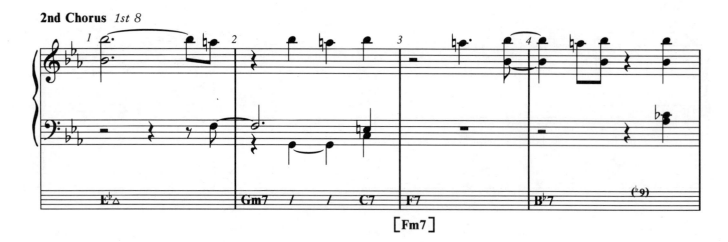
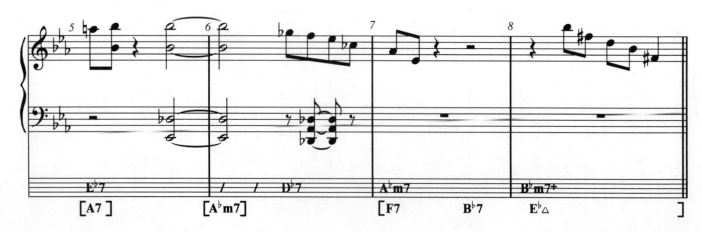

53

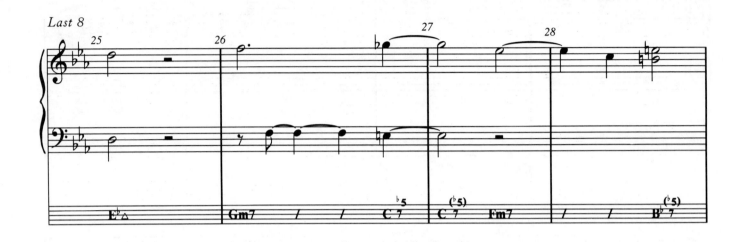

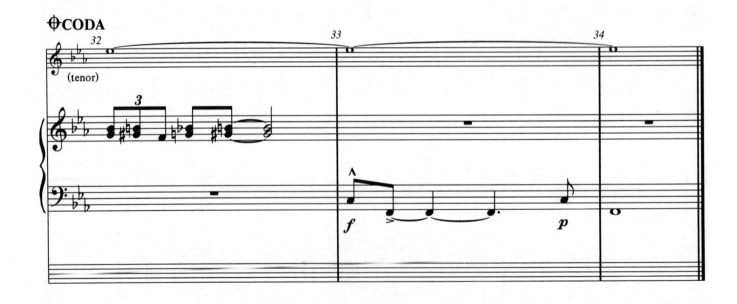

6. PLAYED TWICE

© Copyright 1979 Bocu Music Ltd.

7. CREPUSCULE WITH NELLIE

trans. M. HATHAWAY

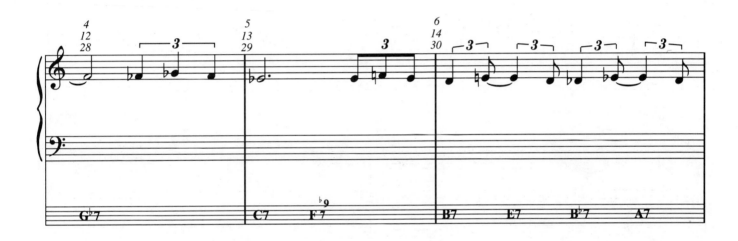
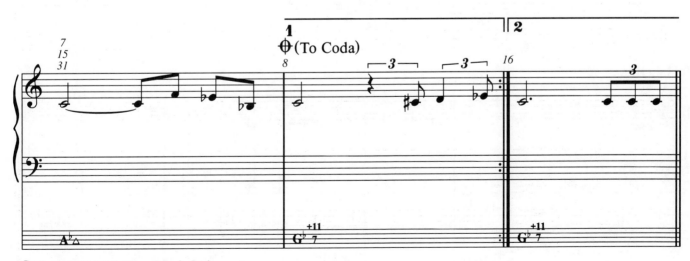

© Copyright 1979 Bocu Music Ltd.

Published by Novello & Company Limited
Music processed by Novello using the Toppan New Scan-Note System
Printed in Great Britain